I0565951

The Land of Possibilities

THE SEARCH FOR GRANDMA LILY

SEREN HART

Second Edition

This book is a work of fiction. Any resemblance to actual events or persons, living or dead, is entirely coincidental.

"The Land of Possibilities," by Seren Hart. Second edition. ISBN 978-1-62137-537-1 (Softcover) 978-1-62137-538-8 (eBook)

Library of Congress Control Number: 2014910889

'Carol' sketch on cover by John LaBerge

Cover Design by K. Cooper of Virtualbookworm.com Publishing

For all souls, especially the littlest of ones...

To my husband, John, and son, Eamon...who inspire me.

To the grace of abundance in simplicity and generosity!

How pleasant will be the family life we shall enjoy for all eternity! While awaiting that blissful eternity, which will open to us soon, since life is but a day, let us work together for the salvation of souls; I of course can do very little, absolutely nothing in fact, alone; what encourages me is the thought that by your side I can be of some use; after all zero, by itself has no value, but put alongside one, it becomes potent, always provided it is put on the proper side after and not before!

~The Little Flower~

ACKNOWLEDGEMENTS

I am grateful for the love of my husband, John Kennedy and my precious son, Nicholas Eamon. The both of you are my inspiration for my very breath. Eamon, I thank you for always keeping your imperfect mom in your heart.

June, you are a true example of a kind neighbor. I thank you for my very first read through and thumbs up…When I re-read the first draft, I did a second draft and a third, etc…finally there was grace! Thank you so much for seeing the potential. Kay and Ivana, I thank you also for your early on read. I hope the end result pleases you both.

Special thanks to all at Virtualbookworm Publishing, Bobby, Kassi and all the staff who helped with my editing, cover design and all my rookie questions. Thanks guys for your patience and caring.

I thank my parents who gave me life through my creator God. Love to my dear siblings, my awesome extended family and loving in-laws and friends. Thank you Holy Trinity, Mary, Angels, Saints and my Christian Catholic faith for being at my side in my constantly evolving spiritual journey, which brought forth *The Land of Possibilities*.

Thanks to all who've ever made me laugh and encouraged the lighter side.

Last but not least…the writers who inspired me.

CONTENTS

THE SEARCH FOR GRANDMA LILY

Second Edition

PROLOGUE

Going into that nightclub was at the time the only thing I could do, and not the least scary thing I did to advance my search for my grandma. I know that sounds weird if you find it hard to identify with grandmas over sixty in nightclubs, but it'll all make sense later.

I'm seventeen...I have a little knowledge of life. Up until the point I'd entered that club, I'd led a fairly normal one—with the emphasis on *fairly*. However, I'd been given no choice to make a life change. The key to all the answers I needed (I thought) was supposedly buried in the wine cellar underneath the nightclub, which would lead me to find out just where my Grandma Lily had disappeared to for the past three or so decades. Now I know this may sound dark, and perhaps just a tiny bit scary, right? But listen, I went through it, and you're just reading it.

Plus, you don't want me to have to hold your hand and blindfold you the whole way. I'm a terrible babysitter. I have my brother Jeremy to attest to that fact.

I felt it was important to tell my story to someone. To anyone who'd listen. Think of it as a long letter to you. I could have tried to find a ghostwriter. I've heard some are really good, but I've just had my fill of strange-sounding titles recently. Ghost...writer? Besides, how could anyone tell my experience as well as I, who was there? I'll try to paint the picture for you as best as I can. I guarantee you won't be bored, and you will

1

want to rescue my grandma even more than me. It's almost like she becomes your grandma too... well, by association.

It's important that I take you back a little. It will help you get to know how it all started and what helped convince me that she was alive. Hopefully by then, you'd also understand my great need and desire to bring her back.

Many would not have thought I'd have mustered up the courage it took to enter that nightclub and the nightmare that awaited me. From kindergarten up until seven years old—it may not seem that long, but take my word, it's a long time when it's happening to you—I was called scaredy cat by the boys and girls at school, no thanks to Jimmy, boy monster. They were right, then, to have that view of me. Wish they could all see me now— or at least read my story. I was always scared up to that point. Luckily for my grandma, my fear or nickname, not necessarily in that order, didn't last.

I remember I'd think to myself back then... I mean kindergarten to seven. No problem, I have undiagnosed ADD too. Even if it was diagnosed, my parents hadn't bought into the whole keep your ADD kids drugged up of the 90's. Anyway, I'd think, what exactly is a scaredy cat? I'd heard they had nine lives. How could the guarantee of nine lives put fear in anything? My parents, on the other hand, never called us names like that. That must have saved me from low, or rather no self-esteem syndrome. My mom always said, "Courage is a great thing, and it pays to be brave." Easier said than done, right? Yeah, you're with me. Besides, paid what? Like a guaranteed monthly salary, no taxes? Yeah, right. Nonetheless, I tried my hardest to live up to that and drown out the other voices...

Then one day it hit me out of nowhere, like a speeding bullet: Ah ha! I'd make believe I really was a cat, but a different kind of cat. Turn the feline name in my favor, with a different adjective: Brave! Now that made sense. At the forefront of my brain would be a courageous cat with the guarantee of nine lives. That's what I was thinking when I entered The Club Monet (the real Monet would be appalled) on 42nd street.

PART ONE

EARTH: CHILDHOOD

ONE

"Wake up, Carol. It's time for school, dear!" came the usual morning shout. I looked up, still very sleepy-eyed, to my mom's face over mine, and of course I was yawning really loudly to make my point. "Oh please, Mom, it's only 7 a.m. Why does school have to start so early? I just want to sleep a bit more. "Now look here young lady—" said my mother Miriam, giving me a stern look.

"I know, I know, stop whining." Putting one leg down after the other, slowly, I got out of bed and headed for the bathroom with my mother in tow, my mind already drifting to the day ahead. Arriving at school was always nerve-racking. What would Jimmy— a skinny, scrawny brat, with a mop of jet black hair—have up his sleeve today? I dreaded to find out. He was the one I had to thank for the 'scaredy cat' nickname. To my dismay, the other kids in my second grade class, other than the little plump twin sisters with matching curly brown hair who felt sorry for me, had followed his popular lead.

An hour later, my mother dropped me off, a three-foot tall kid with tight facial skin, at one of the two elementary schools in Berkeley Springs, West Virginia. My face was especially taut, since my hair was pulled tight into two pigtails, which only enhanced my nervous frame of mind.

I must tell you: I'm an ordinary-looking kid, though my grandma (on my mom's side) thinks I'm cute. She's the one who's around. She couldn't go missing, that'd be pretty hard (I'll explain later). I have bruised cheeks for hours afterwards as proof when she visits.

I arrived at my prison of education. I walked up to my classroom, and for a moment I pretended I lived in this perfect world where everyone is a friend. What an idyllic picture for a second! Literally speaking. For no sooner had I settled in at my desk than I was forced out of my reverie by…who else but Jimmy–boy, the monster. "Hi scaredy cat, look here!"

Caught off guard every time, I turn around and let out a shriek. He was dangling yet another dead or almost-dead mouse. I couldn't quite tell at this angle. "Look at Mickey Mouse," he announced wickedly. Running out of the room, I tumbled into the arms of Mr. Lang, a teacher of the bigger kids (they're at least an inch bigger, anyways). "What's the matter young lady?" he seemed to ask concernedly, looking distressed.

Stammering, I replied, "A deeaaddd mouse."

"A dead mouse is nothing to fear," he said. I was thinking, oh yeah, how would you like to have one appear in your morning cup of coffee? Glad he couldn't read my thoughts or I hoped he couldn't. "Now be a good girl and head back into class," he continued. By then, Ms. Harris was already taking me by the hand, making sure I did just that.

Why did Jimmy seem to dislike me so? I was thinking to myself. Ms. Harris seemed to have taken charge and had Jimmy sitting on his own in the back of the classroom with his hands on the desk. He looked so small and lonely that I felt sorry for him. He wasn't allowed to move those mischievous hands. Why was he so naughty? I'd heard that kids like Jimmy didn't get enough love or attention at home; at least that's what they said on a show my mom was watching on television one morning when I'd had the measles.

The other kids seem to be trying to avoid Jimmy's fate and left me alone.

School was something that was puzzling to me. I couldn't help wondering what it would be like, if I'd been born already knowing everything. Take babies, for instance. How did they know that if they wanted food, they just needed to cry? I'd watch my baby brother Jeremy and marvel. Food: cry, sleep: cry, clean clothes: cry. He knew.

However, there I was, stuck in a classroom with a dead mouse probably sitting in the garbage bin in the corner, who was probably contemplating the next life. The next life for mice! Bet he wished the next life would include becoming Mickey and hanging out at Disneyland. That mouse has it good.

Glancing back once again at Jimmy with his hands still on the desk, I experienced a sudden and surprising, not to mention astounding (enough adjectives? just trying to paint a picture as promised) feeling…words cannot describe it; love flowed through my soul for the enemy, despite the grave wrong. For the first time, I felt courage. Fear also seemed to vanish at that point. Is this where bravery begins?

Powerful! A brave and courageous cat with nine lives! Nothing could stop me now. It could be done.

My father always struck me as one who lived in a unique and mysterious world. To try to figure out what my dad's thinking is like trying to figure out why everything that tastes good is bad for you. My dad Marc's a tall guy with a gangly build and a bald, shaved head. In my mind he's quite handsome, in a sort of ordinary kind of way.

There's really just one thing I want to know from my dad, anyway. All the other questions are simply efforts to trick him.

One morning at breakfast, it was, "Hey Dad, so tell me, what it was like when you were my age and had the measles? You did have the measles, right?" I asked incredulously, hoping he bought it. He knew how my measles last year still haunted me. It's as if speaking of it often would make me believe it happened to someone else.

"Oh yes, I had the measles. It was terribly itchy and uncomfortable," he replied.

"Oh wow!" I answered inappropriately. Multitasking in my thoughts, at eight, was tough. We were nonetheless off to a good start. "So how did Grandma Lily die? Was it from measles too? Do grownups get measles?" I asked without taking a breath. Too excited, I blew it. No transition whatsoever.

My dad never likes to talk about his mom and dad. His face twisted briefly, and he looked like he was about to say something. I was gazing at him so intently you could have waved a rattlesnake in front of my face at that moment and I wouldn't have blinked. Oh, come on Dad, don't clam up please, I was wishing.

"Now, now Caroline..."

I knew the moment was gone when he called me Caroline. It was meant to pacify. Baby brother Jeremy is the one who needs the pacifier, I was thinking, truly annoyed. I knew it was wishful thinking, but I really thought I was going to break ice there.

"Kay, Dad," I replied disappointedly. Then I went off to mope.

Dinner time at my house is pretty comical. We eat quickly. Well, mostly my dad. There was a time he got done in a record three minutes. I was watching the clock facing me on the wall. I think he eats fast because of the way my grandma died, and he thinks I'll eventually get it all out of him if we sit there too long. As always, at dinner he hardly said a word except, "This is really good, Miriam," to my mom. Sometimes I think my mom scares him out of saying anything different. Either that or he's a submissive husband. I'd heard the phrase one Sunday at mass. One night my dad got done with dinner in seven minutes. A record! The beef was really chewy, and we had to chew it or choke. Dad still said it was good.

My mom looks like a beautiful actress someone forgot to cast. My dad doesn't stand a chance. She has sparkling brown eyes that could melt icebergs on a planet where global warming doesn't exist—which also, by the way, will see right through your upcoming fib. Plus a beautiful heart-shaped face that stops traffic. I know you've heard that phrase many times, but I'm the one who literally has to let go of her hand and run away from her when we're crossing the street for fear of losing my young life. Sometimes I stare at myself in the mirror to find some sort of resemblance. That proves very futile, so I give up quickly.

After dinner my dad usually reads me a bedtime story and my mom reads to Jeremy…they actually take turns because I always want the same bedtime story and some nights dad has to double up. Jeremy had absolutely zero interest in my obsession with a certain fairytale. This was usually how it went after dinner. I'll give you an example:

"Kay, Mom, I'm done," I said.

"Very good, honey," replied my mother. "Dad will tuck you in."

"Yes, Mom," I replied, eyeing Dad as we both got up. "Dad, could you read me the story of Grandpa David and Grandma Lily, please?" I asked gently. This was always sensitive territory.

"Sure, honey," he replied. These were his only spoken words since 'grace.' How good the dinner was didn't count. That didn't ring true to my mostly baby teeth. Though, of course, I was grateful. It beat starving. My mom couldn't cook to save her life. I'd heard that when she and my dad met in college, she ate mostly cereal. My mom studied psychology but worked as a personal assistant most of my life. She often joked that psychology was a hobby that had helped her figure out her oh-so-interesting husband and children, so she was grateful for her years in college. However, for cooking there was no family gene. This was also an early warning to any suitors in my future.

TWO

I cuddled up in my little bed, which I hoped someone would notice at some point that I was outgrowing, since my feet dangled over the edge. As my dad sat down to read, I was excited and in heavy anticipation, though it'd been the same story for the past year. I was hoping some new information would escape.

I had to get to the whole truth at some point. I knew it was just a matter of time till I'd be grown up and be able to make my own schedule and do my own research. Having to account for my whereabouts at all times at eight years old wasn't helping at all.

"Tonight we have the short version, sweetheart okay? It's been a long day," said my dad to me. He began…

"Once upon a time, there was a young woman turning sixteen years old. To her, this was the biggest event ever of her life. She had dreamed of her first kiss, and she'd heard that's when she'd have it."

Okay, Dad, move on from the mushy stuff was what I thought to myself. He always began it like a fairytale, but for me it was way deeper than that. Though I also refer to it as the fairytale story, it isn't. It's as true as you and I.

And so the story goes…

The home of Lily Brandt, Riverside, Wyoming ~ 1948

(Once upon a time, there was a young woman named Lily...)

"Coming, Mother!" I yell. "It's my birthday you know," I continue, laughing out loud.

"Yes, I know, but we still have so much to do for your party this evening. Your last-minute mother still hasn't ordered your cake!"

"That's okay, Mother. As long as we have sixteen candles, we can squeeze them all onto a cupcake, for all I care!"

My mother, Mary, laughs. It's a great big belly laugh. A laugh like that is never late.

I look at my reflection coming down the stairway. What a gorgeous dress Mother picked out. Full skirt, pretty pink roses over lilac, my favorite colors, I think admiringly. And the pink pumps are just divine, and oh, how I love those pink daffodils Mom chose for my hair.

My father was killed in the war when I was only nine years old. Wish he was here to see me tonight. Dad was so handsome, and David is the picture of him at seventeen. The resemblance is startling.

When David arrives at my party, all the girls rush toward him drooling, but he has eyes for only me, and he's looking in my direction. He walks across the room to me, then stops and smiles, looking down at me. He is so tall.

"Happy sweet sixteen, Lily," he says.

"Thanks, David," I reply a bit nervously. "How was your drive out to the country?" David lived over in the city of Casper. We only saw each other in the summers now, when his parents took him back here. They'd relocated there when he was nine for his dad's work. Rural Wyoming wasn't his lifestyle anymore.

"I ran across the deer, the antelopes, and the cows. The usual," he says with laughter in his voice. I was drifting, thinking about my first kiss and getting gooey inside.

"Oh yeah, don't you just love God's creatures?" I really truly mean that, though I have no idea why I'm saying that right now.

David continues, "Beautiful birthday cake, but not as beautiful as you."

I can barely look up. I'm melting into popcorn butter. "Oh yeah, I like it too... I mean, thank you." Nerves are in full glory. "It's weird what my mother can accomplish at the last minute." I answer with a nervous laugh.

"Shall we dance, princess?" David is such a great dancer. The waltz is my favorite. Mother must have seen us glide to the dance floor. The music started as soon as his hands reached for mine. So we dance, and everyone in the room vanishes. It's my first grownup dance. I have no idea what grownups make of 16-year-olds, but I feel grown up right now.

"So David, I've chosen you to cut my birthday cake. Aren't you lucky?" That was my sorry attempt at flirtation, to hide my nerves, of course.

He bursts out laughing.

"What's funny? Are you too much of a grownup to cut cake with a 16-year-old?" I ask him teasingly. "What's so funny about me asking you to cut my birthday cake? You said it was beautiful and, to quote you exactly, not as beautiful as me. Don't you want the attention, is that it? I know you don't like parties and you must be here only because of me. Did your mom and dad pressure you? Are you here out of obligation?" This is not going well. I can't stop talking. To make it worse I'm also rambling, I can tell. That's bound to be a turn-off. I'm literally kissing my first kiss goodbye.

"Easy, easy, you're on a roll, princess. Have I ever refused you anything since we were toddlers? Even let you have some of my rocky road ice cream. Remember that?

I can't help but crack up laughing. This is why I love David. He always knows how to lighten a moment. I noticed my mother waving and clapping in my direction at the other end of the room, trying to grab my attention. The cutting of a sweet sixteen's birthday cake, is a big moment. My mother already knew that I was going to ask David and considering none of the other girls were in his arms at the moment (which could change in an instant the way they were all ogling at him) it was good timing.

Finally! I'm thinking to myself, still trying hard to conceal as well as contain my excitement and nervous anticipation. A bit apprehensively, I approach my butterfly cake with its sixteen candles. It's glowing. Everyone's gathered around me. I close my eyes to make my wish. I pray David doesn't go to any wars. I also wish my dad was here—he'd been gone for seven years— so that's not a realistic wish. Then I blow out the candles.

David and I cut my cake, and we each take a bite. I could hear the drum rolls, first-kiss thoughts pounding loudly in my head. I swear I thought I'd pass out. My heart rate was so fast.

Then something like a feather brushed my forehead, and then it was over.

I almost thought the butterfly cake had come alive and flew over me. No such thing. Soon afterwards, the party ended with bombshell, life-of-the-party, Meredith in David's arms.

With everyone gone, my mom and I are both exhausted. I'm also hugely disappointed. My mom decides to put just a 'few' things away tonight and asks me to keep her a little company, though I'm not allowed to do any cleaning since it's my big day. I wish I could get out of the keeping company as I did the cleaning and sneak quietly to my room to be alone, but that would seem so ungrateful after everything she's done for the party.

"Enjoyed the party, sweetheart?" she asks.

"Yes, Mother, it was great. Thank you so much," I reply as I hug her.

She adds astutely, "You seem far away. Is everything alright?"

See why I wanted to sneak to my room? "Why do you say that?" I reply guardedly, looking away.

"Oh, nothing, it's just that you're awfully quiet for such a fun night. You don't get to be sweet sixteen ever again you know!"

I want to laugh and cry at the same time. Instead I say, "It was fun mother, thank you." I didn't want to hurt her feelings.

"So you're happy?"

"Wish dad was here tonight." That's a true statement and will get the attention elsewhere.

"Yeah, I know, honey. You wished your dad was here tonight. But we know he was, we still feel his presence, don't we?" My mom's pretty big on everyone who's died still being around in the spiritual sense and sometimes I do feel like my dad is watching over me. It's hard to explain. So I agree.

"Yes Mother, I do." I answer. My father was killed in Pearl Harbor. I despise wars. I don't know how anyone thought they helped anyone.

My 'bummed out first kiss blues' secret's safe. Or so I think. She has no idea? Not so quick.

"So everything went as you'd have liked, dear?" asks my mom again, not letting up. I'm thinking she can read me like a book.

This time I decide to not say a word. She drops it.

"Well, dear, if you would like to talk about it sometime, I'm here." I smile at her. The mood's lighter. She says, "Did you see Mr. and Mrs. Jamieson? They actually danced!" The Jamieson's were the only grownup couple friends of my mom who were invited. Mrs. Jamieson and my mom had been friends, well from birth you could say. Their mothers were friends and gave birth to each a few days apart.

"No Mother, I missed that" I say a bit absentmindedly, wondering what else I'd missed of my party, caught up in first-kiss blues.

I go to bed that night hoping that David won't be sent off to any wars. He had enlisted in the US army. I'm hoping we marry before any war breaks out and he has to leave. Of course we'll also have five babies right away. I love David and intend to marry him, sweet sixteen kiss or not.

Two years later after fending off the likes of Meredith and company on David's future visits and world wars we got married on my eighteenth birthday to the day. It was a joyous occasion and all my mother's adult couple friends were invited this time. We remain in Riverside. I found out David never actually cared too much for the city life. As neither did I. Two years later our son was born.

That was my version of Cinderella. My dad says that's all he knows of the story of his parents when they were young. He calls it the short version. I knew it was also the fairytale version, but I didn't know if he knew that I knew it was. I'd also never had the long version, so him calling it the short version, was just plain silly.

Sometimes I made up my own continuations where Grandma Lily got her other four, and visited with us every weekend. That was my fairytale ending.

I'd heard my parents speaking when I was five years old when I'd walked into their bedroom to ask for milk, because I couldn't sleep. The monsters had woken me up. I've had monsters in my dreams for as long as I could remember. They weren't really bad monsters. They were more like, annoying and sometimes kept me awake. Lately they'd been around almost every night as if on a mission.

I heard my mom say "Marc you know what it's like, when you were a boy you were in an orphanage." I had no idea what they were speaking of. I found out years later that my parents were considering adopting an orphan and that's how the subject had begun.

I'd asked, "What's an orpanish?" I couldn't pronounce it of course.

My parents were taken aback that I'd bumped in at that particular moment.

"It's where kids who have no moms and dads live," said my mom.

"No moms or dads?" I asked astonishingly.

"Yes, honey," replied my mom.

"Daddy was one of these kids?" I asked, quite astutely for a five year old. The answer was yes. "Why?" I ask. The most dreaded of questions for parents.

Then he proceeded to tell the awful story of when he was a young boy of around seven years old and he was taken into the orphanage. Then he also told me the first story of his parents when they were young and that had become the bedtime story. I must say I liked the latter much better than the former...the fairytale eased the sadness a bit.

My dad must have thought that he'd been given no choice at that time but to come up with some kind of fairytale story to ease my pain, after they'd told me the heartbreaking news of my other half of my tree. I'd just walked in at the wrong moment and heard something that I wasn't supposed to know about.

I really don't think he was trying to get me to think of romance at five. Yuck, anyway. As if, was what I'd thought back then. That's why I never liked Cinderella, Sleeping Beauty or any of those fairy tales. Most parents that read those to their five year olds are just setting them up for premature adolescence. Anyway, I really just loved hearing about my lost grandparents. It's the only consolation I felt when thinking of them. It made me happy to hear about them in some way. Sometimes I wonder if my dad made it all up but since he's a truthful person I have to believe what he'd said, that Grandma Lily had told him this story when she was alive and he was a boy and to this day he never forgot. However, it seemed that whatever had happened to him in the orphanage had erased much of his later childhood memories, because he said they were all very vague.

After I crawled into bed with my parents, the monsters again returned in my dreams. There were the usual three of them, and mostly all they do is grin, laugh and chatter among themselves in words I do not understand. But tonight for the first time they added words I did understand. They were repeating over and over again, "Grandma, grandma, grandma. Alive!

I woke up yet again, in a cold sweat, my heart pounding.

"The monsters, they say Grandma's alive!" I yell out to my parents. This is the first time I understood anything they've said! Usually it's just chatter, grinning and laughing!"

"It's okay, baby, it's just a dream," said my mom to me in her attempts to curb my feverish excitement.

"I know but they said Grandma Lily's alive!" I say to my dad hoping he'll believe it, since I had no luck with my mother.

"As your mom said Caroline. It was just a dream, now try to go back to sleep," he replied. No luck there either. They both clearly didn't believe me or the credibility of the monsters.

The next night the monsters returned, again chattering about Grandma Lily being alive. I no longer ran to my parents. That had been proven useless. I felt for sure in my soul that my grandma was alive, and I had to find her for my dad. The little blue monsters were my friends now and I finally knew why they'd always been around. They'd been waiting to deliver a message. An extremely important one!

THREE

Three years later, they returned.

I think they believed if they stay away completely I will forget about Grandma Lily. They are so wrong. I'd actually missed them and it was so comforting last night in my dream. They were chatting about Grandma Lily to me and at one time I could have sworn they were trying to tell me where to find her. Then I woke up.

However I was paying dearly for all of it right now.

I'd woken up even more drained than usual and I could barely keep my eyes open at school. Though it was never a nightmare while they were around, the next day was—well, a day-mare, to be exact. I hadn't got any sleep and thoughts of Grandma Lily were haunting my thoughts today.

"Carol you're nodding off. Pay attention dear," rattled Ms. Gilroy. She's really kind, and pretty too, although the kids said she was like a hundred years old but had stopped aging. It was hard to tell if she was older than my mother. I asked her once, "How old are you, Ms. Gilroy? Are you older than my mom?"

"Sweetheart, I don't know. I've stopped counting and I have no clue how old your mom is," she replied.

Hmmm, I thought, quite an evasive answer. Clearly one hundred years old. I agree with the other kids.

I was jerked back to the present. "I'm sorry Ms. Gilroy, didn't sleep well last night. I'll try to stay awake," I said to her, rubbing my eyes to make the point. Jimmy scowled at me. What now? I really didn't need his tricks today. He was looking really well put together, and even his hair was combed. I hoped he'd behave today. I wasn't feeling up to dealing with his tricks.

That wish was short-lived—lasted until recess. Brittany and Karen, the 'twins,' and I were having our Nutella sandwiches which beats peanut butter and jelly any day. Then, incoming Jimmy and his two buddies in crime, Kobe and Lake. Jimmy was the leader.

"Hey, Jimmy, having mice for lunch today?" I asked jokingly, reveling in my newfound courage. Brittany and Karen roared with laughter. They really were my biggest fans, those two. Who am I kidding? My only fans, but who needs more than two firm friends (When all you have, is two).

I'd have liked Jimmy too, actually, if he'd start behaving.

"Ha-ha, funny, funny," he said as he ran up to me and tugged at one of the ribbons in my hair, and then took off with Kobe and Lake in tow. My hair ribbon was ruined. They were my favorite ones, too. My only one with lace. Total day-mare.

"He really likes you, he's just a silly boy," remarked Karen.

"My mom got these in the Main, and she only goes there once a year with my godmother," I moaned.

"You still have one good one left," murmured Karen. "Maybe you can wear one pigtail."

I usually had two pigtails, my preferred look, so that wasn't much consolation. But I couldn't blame her for trying.

"Change my look? Why what's wrong with having the same one?" I was curious now.

"I heard someone say change is good," she declared, all grown-uppity.

"Who?"

"An old wife," she replied.

I was still distressed. "An old wife?" I muttered, eyeing her quizzically.

"An old wife's tale."

Having never heard of something so ridiculous, I chuckled, feeling better already.

"I wish he knew how upset it's going to make my mom and then when she tells his mom about his little dirty tricks," I said, sighing.

Brittany, not letting this pass since it was the first time she'd heard me 'threatening to tell,' perked up. "Are you going to tell your mom?" she asked, flabbergasted and looking at me in disbelief.

She was right on. You must know that I've been protecting Jimmy all this time. But for a moment I was tempted.

"Naah…"

We headed back to class.

The day-mare got worse. It was math time.

"Okay, everyone, homework please," said Ms. Gilroy, eyeing me instantly. I was famous for not doing math homework. Not my favorite subject. Who invented it? Looking at my blank answers next to the multiple choice questions, I wondered if I could quickly shade some answers in. It was multiple-choice and no one ever said it was a sin to guess anything.

Then I was saved. Someone else was grabbing her attention. She'd shifted to Jimmy—I lucked out big time! I saw Jimmy beaming confidently. "I did all mine, Ms. Gilroy!" he said.

"All right, Jimmy. I don't just want to know the answer. Come up to the board and show us how you did it. We'll start with number three."

By the look on Jimmy's face, I was thinking his confidence was totally misguided. I didn't think he was expecting that. He must have been a multiple-choice guesser as well. At that moment for the very first time, we'd established common ground. Jimmy walked up to the board, a bit wobbly, not so confident anymore. He got to the board, took a piece of chalk, and did what looked like a Greek calculation, even to me.

The look on Ms. Gilroy's face said it all.

"I didn't get to do this one, Ms. Gilroy, because I ran out of fingers and toes," Jimmy stammered, squirming from the looks on our faces and breaking out into a furious sweat. The kids roared laughter and made me feel sorry for him, even though he was always mean to me. Kobe and Lake hid their faces in a book.

Thanks to Jimmy's little mishap, we got dismissed early. Ms. Gilroy developed a sudden headache. Yaay! We all yelled as we ran out. My day-mare was cut short. I was saved twice today by my so-called enemy.

EARTH: TEEN YEARS

FOUR

Meanwhile, by seventh grade, Jimmy and I were firm friends. How did it happen? Well, it's quite simple. He proved harmless, his pranks weren't worth telling on, and dead mice no longer scared me. That wasn't a challenge for him any more...and most importantly, we grew up! Being mean to a girl was no longer cool. The former mischievous infant brat was now also the cool almost teen that stood up for weaker kids when he saw them being picked on.

Being thirteen, to me, felt pretty weird. I was stuck between just yesterday asking where babies come from, and not being to make my own schedule to continue my research. My dad was still an enigma (grown-up word). See what I mean? And I was too old for what I loved most—the bedtime story—and Dad still spoke only like three words a day. Once a month I was able to somehow open a discussion around it, keep and see what else I can gather.

I found him in his La-Z-Boy, reading his latest sports illustrated. My dad's a sports writer. I was also harboring a secret, not that I'd tell my parents anyway. Last night the blue monsters made a singing announcement. They were for the first time ever, not grinning or chatting but singing. An old song I'd heard my mom play on the CD player before called New York, New York! And that's all they did! They just sang that song over and over again. So I believe that's where Grandma Lily might be. This is such exciting news. I can barely breathe.

I can't let this even accidentally slip out. If I do I fear they will try to stop me from ever going to New York. I know it. They already feel that my obsession with Grandma Lily is unhealthy. So I will keep my secret.

"Hi Dad, what's new in the world of sports these days?" I asked, feigning some interest but really looking for an opening.

"Uh-huh."

Dad, I know that last month…" I stressed on the last month part so he'd know how long it'd been. "…when we spoke about Grandma Lily, you mentioned that remembering when you were a boy she dressed up a lot in beautiful fancy clothes? Do you think she and your dad went to a lot of parties?" I bemused, grasping at straws, not sure where I was headed. It was always a shot in the dark.

"They might have," was his reply.

"Grown up parties are boring. All that standing around and yelling above the loud noise to strange people." Once said, I began to question if my view was maybe just a little bit premature because of my first big party experience. That's what they seemed like to me, though. My mom had taken us to work with her one day when she was helping serve at a party for my godmother Lady Hall — whom my mom works with as her personal assistant. They always say work with each other not for, since they're such close friends.

My dad was out of town covering a sports event and there was no one to babysit us. I remember sneaking out of the room I was supposed to be asleep in and standing above the staircase, looking down. Who could sleep in that kind of racket? Noticing a fruit punch bowl, while no one noticed me, I ventured down to the party and helped myself to some of it. One good thing here, I was thinking. Those little tiny pieces of black eggs on crackers I noticed my mom passing around on a tray looked so gross. Shortly thereafter, I passed out at the top of the stairs where I'd return to sit and sip and continue to observe. No one had seen me until after the party and I guess they thought I'd just taken a walk and sat there and fallen asleep. Years later I mentioned it to my mother and I found out it was an alcoholic punch. My mom, lucky for her, escaped CPS, though for me, not so sure.

"Maybe not so boring, if you like that kind of thing," my dad remarked, closing his eyes for a second—but not too quick that I didn't notice.

Feeling him closing up, I moved quickly. "Do you think they went to a lot of parties?" I ask him.

"Just a feeling," he said guardedly.

"Oh yeah?" I pressed.

I always say that when contemplating my next move. Or running out of time.

"Come on, dear, let's go set your mom free from the kitchen," he said.

We silently make our way to my mother in the kitchen, both lost in our thoughts. I was wondering if Grandma Lily may have been a Manhattan society lady?

On arrival in the kitchen, I noticed my mother didn't seem to be her usual perky self. "What's wrong, Mom?" I asked.

"Oh, just heard you and your dad in there. I wish you weren't so obsessed with your Grandma Lily."

"Sorry Mom, I reply I just have a strong feeling that she's alive and..."

Raising her hand to silence me "Uh uh...enough dear. Remember some things we may never get answers to."

I was thinking differently on this one. "Yes, Mom," I replied. In a way I'm really glad she interrupted me. What if New York had slipped out?

Lightening things up, she smiled. "I've made your favorite dish—Manhattan clam chowder. Let's eat."

I smiled as well, thinking, now why has that always been my favorite soup? I was momentarily consoled. If my mother only knew.

❁❁❁

"Miriam, I need you in here, dear!" was the request coming from the huge study library that belonged in a British museum. Lady Hall was a transplant to America from London England, although sometimes she'd wished she wasn't. Lady Hall didn't favor her British roots too much. At least, not since she'd become an American citizen some forty years ago and would not let anyone forget it. Pity she couldn't lose the accent. Her only drawback, she'd say. Miriam had been Lady Hall's assistant for the past 15 years.

"I'll be right there, Liz! The scones are almost done," shouted Miriam, trying her best to juggle the many demanding tasks of Lady Hall. Ouch, grazing her hand on the hot oven. She rushed to the freezer to put some ice on it. Miriam did not like burn marks.

"Here I am!" she said to Lady Hall. "Was there something you needed?" Miriam asked sincerely. She really cared about Lady Hall, and as Lady Hall often said to her scrabble-playing friends, "I'm quite fond of my Miriam." It was a long run from the kitchen. Though claiming to no longer be English, Lady Hall still believed in castles, though mini ones. A bit out of breath, Miriam entered the library and asked again, "Was there something you needed, Liz? I'm sorry I couldn't get here any faster—"

Interrupting her by sneezing and talking at the same time, Ms. Hall said, "Sweetheart, I never call for no reason. It's quite certain I need something. How are those scones coming? I believe it's almost time for tea. I shouldn't have any, I gather, with this dreadful cold. Ah-choo! Excuse me dear, it's quite horrible to be sick and old. Pray you never become an old lady."

That garnered a laugh from Miriam. "I'll do my best. Now, what can I get you? The scones are ready now and you are not that old."

"Well, let's have them while they're hot, and I'll have some Earl Grey today, I believe," she said, and then pondered for a moment. "But wait, I called you in for a reason. Oh, I'm becoming senile, dear. Ah-choo! Pass me a nappy. Oh, I remember, I couldn't find a single nappy or tissue in here, and we must have a bit of a chat about Caroline. It's been some time since we've discussed the girl and it's getting so close, and is Marc still moping around hoping for another child? That's just absurd. Jeremy's barely out of his nappies, and if he only knew what's in store for you, he'd stop walking around with that gloomy face."

"You know as well as I do that's not the only reason for his gloom and he's just taking it hard what the doctors have said about us having more children,"

"I've never believed a thing that lot has said. Always diagnosing me with this or that which is hardly ever accurate and I bet I'll outlive the lot of them. Thank you, dear." She reached for the napkin. "It's quite magical how you find things. I believe I'm becoming as blind as an old bat. Where are those scones?"

"I'll go get them," said Miriam.

FIVE

There's something unsound about waking up early on Saturday mornings with no need to, but Saturdays always caught me unaware. I always promised myself I'd sleep till noon. It never happened. I'd been programmed by Monday through Friday. To make up, I vowed to not leave my room before then. I'd wake up, but would not descend to the rest of humanity until after the noon hour.

By then, my mom would be out in the garden tending her roses and my dad swinging out on the porch in the swing chair, reading his latest Sports Illustrated. He'd be finished with the paper probably since 7 a.m. He's always an early bird who catches the worm. I could see my brother Jeremy feeding the chickens. It's his favorite thing to do.

I plopped down next to my dad on the swing chair. "Sleep well, honey?"

"Yeah, pretty good, Dad."

"I took down a pretty squeaky clean breakfast tray around ten. You must have been up early."

Gotta love my parents. They put my breakfast in a tray outside my door every Saturday morning, and I put it back out when I'm done so they'd know I'm alive.

"Was huungry," I said stressing on the word to make my point.

"The tray gave that away. So, how did you spend the last three hours?"

"Well, Dad, you know…the usual." I joined him on the porch swing. "Morning prayers…" I glanced over, making sure he's heard. That's their one rule for my morning indulgence is I promise to pray my morning prayers, especially the rosary. My mother says if it wasn't for the Blessed Virgin I wouldn't even be here…there was some sort of miracle when she was in labor with me. The details I never got, not that I minded. So anyway, that was probably why I really felt close to the Blessed Virgin Mary and actually enjoyed praying the Holy Rosary. I continued with my morning recap "…one hour dance, one hour talking with friends, homework forty-five minutes, and cleaning the room, fifteen minutes." Not necessarily in that order of course. By the way, Brittany and I pretty much completed our homework together by phone, so you can include some bonus homework time in talking with friends."

Dad gave me a weird smile, which made me feel a little uncomfortable and then went back into sports heaven.

By the way, if I haven't mentioned Brittany, Karen, Jimmy and I are now all dancers.

Brittany and Karen's parents had put them in dance mainly so they'd lose weight and now they were as lean as anything and amazing classical dancers. Jimmy was always skinny and lean so what was his reason? I have no idea. But he was good. So good.

I'd joined classical dance class with Brittany, Karen and Jimmy, when I'd figured it was probably a great way to get to New York. I found out through Brittany that all the top dance schools were there and if I got really good I could convince my parents to let me move there after I graduated. I still had a ways to go to catch up with the three of them but I was working really hard. I had actually grown to love it and I was getting really good.

Our dance troupe rehearsed Saturday afternoons from 4–6. It was perfect—didn't interfere with my Saturday morning indulgence.

Today was a perfect day. I was swinging, singing and humming. I like humming much better than singing, mostly because I hardly remember the words of songs, and we danced classical so there were no words there, either. My godmother Lady Hall has already offered to pay for a fancy dance school in New York. I mean, she's really rich, at least by our standard. She's a good soul and very generous, my mom says. Although, I'd heard at church about her not being able to enter heaven very easily. It was the camel and the needle story. Somehow I think she'd make it.

Okay, Dad was a little boring at the moment stuck in his magazine. I could have sat there for the next two hours, and with his head in that magazine there'd be nothing. Bonding time was about up. Better go see what my mom had growing. I was feeling refreshed and ready for some good conversation.

"Hey, Mom, how's the Garden of Eden this morning?" I approached her laughingly. My mother's rose garden was a true work-of-art. She had roses of every color of the rainbow and they made the most beautiful kaleidoscope. "How do you get the most beautiful roses on the planet mom?" I asked her enthusiastically

"By descending a bit earlier than noon on Saturday mornings, is how I get it done," she replied as she hugged me, trying not to get soil all over my clean clothes. "Good afternoon."

"'Kay Mom, got it, afternoon," I answered, laughing. I was in a good mood. Nothing could stop me. "I love Saturdays!" I yelled at the top of my lungs to no one in particular. My mom totally ignored me, as if I didn't just yell out at the top of my lungs. She was examining a rose like a physicist.

"Spoke to Brittany's mom earlier. She says your school troupe will be performing in June at the playhouse, is that right?"

"Geez, I must have forgotten to tell you. Intentionally so I wouldn't feel the pressure." I kidded.

We'd already been rehearsing like mad for it. The routine was coming along great. Other than dancer extraordinaire Jimmy, who'd almost broke my arm last Saturday, which I left out.

"Classical dance is awesome, Mom!" I added after a moment's thought.

That was the most excited I'd ever sounded about dance. It was my ticket to New York. I had to be careful, though, and not blow my cover. If I was too excited about New York, and not just about dance, it might seem suspicious. Only I and the blue monsters knew. Not even Brittany, Jimmy or Karen had a clue. "You're really into it, aren't you sweetie? That's really neat to see you passionate and excited about it," she added, looking at me a bit suspiciously I thought. Perhaps I'm just paranoid. After dance rehearsal, Mom took all four of us out to ice cream at Bonnie's Best, the local ice cream parlor, for our post-grueling treat. Dance class was really tough today. Gosh!

My mom never cooked on Saturdays. Saturday was our night out or take-out "in" night. Either way, there was no cooking going on, which was fine with me! Tonight it was pizza, take-in. My mom and dad had barbeque chicken pizza, and now seven year old Jeremy and I shared a small Hawaiian, except his half was without the ham. I must say he was different. Sometimes it seemed he was nothing like the rest of us especially me. He was always so amazingly transparent. He didn't have any secrets. He was also a vegetarian at seven.

"May I be excused to my room now, Mother, Father?" he said, looking at both of them in turn. "The pizza was delicious, and I thank you for being my mother and father. I'd like to go to my room now and watch cartoons, please? Thanks."

I mean, who speaks like that? Please and thanks together. He's a genius. He was projecting beforehand to get his way. Wish I was that smart at seven. Who am I kidding? Wish I was that smart now.

"Okay darling. Don't you feel well? You aren't coming down with something, are you? Tonight I thought we'd watch you and Carol's favorite Christmas movie, 'The Night before Christmas,'" said my mother.

"Well, all right, Mom, I feel fine" he replied after a slight hesitation. "That sounds good. Hope Carol doesn't talk too much, like always during the movie. I like to focus."

I stuck my tongue out. "And Mr. Polite, if you can refrain from crying every five, we have a deal." With that comment he looked like he was about to, and the movie hadn't even started.

I felt really ashamed to hurt his feelings. After all, I was the older one. "Sorry, Jeremy, didn't mean it." How could I taunt a seven-year-old vegetarian, especially when I could have prevented it? I get the feeling whenever anyone's eating chicken he still got queasy? I remember vividly the night two years ago when Jeremy announced he was going to be a vegetarian, although he'd called it vegetation for a while there. 'Tarian' wasn't rolling off his five–year-old tongue.

That day, he'd put two and two together about chicken dinner. We'd all sat down to eat. He ran into the room, quite distressed and out of breath. "Dale's missing!" Dale was his chicken. Though I'd known about Dale, I hadn't told my parents—not intentionally, just not in time to save her. Go figure out the name Dale for a hen. Jeremy was thinking she was a boy, I guess. I didn't have the heart to tell him Dale was a girl. I guess a girl could be called Dale but I knew he thought it was a boy because I'd heard him refer to Dale as he.

We'd been getting eggs from "Dale" and our other five hens as long as I could remember. Dad had decided that we weren't going to farm the chickens for eggs anymore. When he'd got home that evening from work he'd decided that Dale was dinner, quite unaware of the friendship that had been forming between his son and Dale. It was quite cute to see Jeremy call out to her and feed her corn and rice grains. No doubt at those times my dad was watching sports. Men tend to miss out on important events around those times. Then again my dad had a good excuse, since it's his job.

Jeremy knew Dale well. Although all the chickens were all the same white color and looked the same to me, he'd identified some special mark that none of the other chickens had. He'd gone to wish Dale goodnight, right as we were about to sit down for dinner around six. Chickens tend to sleep right as dinner starts—maybe it's their method of escaping what's going on inside. However it doesn't explain them being awake at lunch. Guess they can't sleep all day. Though, I would.

"Who's Dale, honey?" my mom asked innocently. She thought she knew all his friends by name.

"Dale's my chicken! I went to wish him goodnight but he wasn't there." Then the bawling had started. Dale was in a dish, already cut into legs, thighs, wings and breasts. He'd been the first one to go.

Jeremy had never made the association with Dale's family and what we ate. My mom was pretty shaken up, I could tell, trying to stop the howling.

"Mom, I'd like to go to my room, please? I'd just like cereal tonight," I said. This was too painful to watch. I made my exit. Next day I heard from Jeremy that dad said Dale had not been a pet but food to nourish us. Jeremy didn't buy it. He'd been a 'vegetation' ever since. As for me, I joined in solidarity with my brother and stopped eating chicken. Well, only for a few days.

Jeremy also stopped eating eggs, so he's really 'almost' a vegan, since he still drinks cow's milk and cheese—but vegan, though easier to pronounce is probably a little too advanced a concept for him to grasp, I think.

Somewhere out there, Dale's having sweet dreams in chicken heaven. Though it didn't explain the fact that my parents ate him that night, that's where I told Jeremy that Dale was. He seemed okay with that. It was the least I could do to alleviate my guilt of not saving Dale. My mom tried to salvage hers, too. Next day she brought home a kitten.

🝰🝰🝰

"Two days 'til Christmas, Mom, can't wait to see Grandma Julie and Grandpa Dwayne!" I said excitedly.

"Yes me too. They make Christmas even more fun, don't they, dear?"

"Uh-huh," I replied.

"Hope Grandpa Dwayne dresses up as Saint Nick," said Jeremy. There's never been any doubt in our minds where our Christmas presents came from. Our parents told us Santa Claus did not come down the chimney and I was okay with that. When the kids at school talked about Santa's presents after Christmas, I looked away and kept silent not to burst their bubble and be a joy stealer.

Bingo! He did. "Well, I have a surprise for you two. Dad is going to dress up like Saint Nick on Christmas this year, and he's going to wear the beard and everything."

Geez, Mom, ruin the surprise, I was thinking

"Really, Mom?" yelled Jeremy. Gosh, the kid was loud, barely holding in his excitement. "Can't wait to see what dad will look like!"

"As long as we don't forget where our presents come from," I added wryly. Now I seemed to be a joy stealer. Well if we aren't supposed to believe Santa brought presents I was going to make sure we kept it in perspective and our heads out of the clouds. I mean, the chimney.

"Well, since it's Dad dressing up like him, maybe we can play along this time," my mom said, winking at us.

"Cool!" Jeremy yelled. This time, even louder.

Christmas was a very special time for us with the only grandparents we'd ever known. My mom's mom and dad. They always arrived two days before Christmas, and left two days after. I always looked forward to their visit. We only saw them once at Christmas which just isn't enough, considering they're doubling up for the other lost grandparents and our parents were both only children, so we had no uncles or aunts. Deprived.

I could do more of my own thing, when they were here for Christmas. My parents were a little less absorbed with their children. Last Christmas while they were here I even made a great find. I found a picture of a young woman that looked a lot like Dad. She had his exact eyes and I was praying to high heaven it was Grandma Lily. I so wanted to see what she'd looked like and dad didn't have any pictures. I showed it to my dad and he almost flipped! He yelled yes even louder than Jeremy at his loudest! It was the only one he'd had when he'd been brought to the orphanage and he'd thought it was lost forever. He hadn't seen it since he was around seven years old. My dad and I bonded really tight that Christmas. Grandma Lily was a pretty, petite woman and what was really ironic is she looked almost exactly like me. Dad had said before that I looked like her and he was right.

I was hoping I got lucky again this Christmas and found something else down there. I was previously not allowed in the basement but when I brought the picture my dad was so excited it was like he forgot I wasn't supposed to be down there. Well, for as long as his excitement lasted. After which it was back under lock and key. A regular Fort Knox. I have no idea where I could find anything now. I just hope and keep my eye out.

"They're here!" yelled my mom as she saw my grandparents pulling up to our house in their old blue station wagon. Why does everyone yell at holidays? I was thinking. We all ran out to greet them with my dad, trailing behind. He's the only one holding it in. I haven't seen him show any excitement since my Grandma Lily's photo was found. Although I must say he and my Grandpa Dwayne usually have a great time together.

"My, my how much you've grown!" exclaimed Grandma Julie (what was she wearing?) as she got out of the car in a rush to hug me. It looked like Grandpa Dwayne was still attempting to park (highly unsafe) and Grandma Julie had to get out before he closed her in on her side. My grandpa claims to have been a racecar driver in his day. Convince me please, someone. I just can't picture it.

"Geez, thanks, Grandma," I replied. It had to be true—she said it every year, and then we'd go to the store to get new clothes. She heralded in my growth.

"You too grandma."

Her hair was now completely white since last Christmas.

"Oh dear, I've stopped growing," she laughed. "Just didn't use the hair dye this time."

It was Jeremy's turn to be hugged. He did not like to be hugged by Grandma Julie…well, he didn't mind the hug, but the lifting off his feet bothered him. She's fairly strong for her age.

Trying to avoid the inevitable, Jeremy angled toward my grandpa for a more manlike greeting. "Hi there, champ," he said, patting Jeremy on the head. "How's my vegetarian these days?" he asked, looking down on Jeremy like a giant. He's 6'5." Don't know how he ever fit into those tiny little race cars.

Jeremy beamed. "Just great grandpa, mom discovered tofu, plenty of protein." He flexed his tiny arms to prove it. Highly entertaining, especially to Grandpa Dwayne, who chuckled.

"How are you today grandpa?" Jeremy continued in painfully proper speech.

Before he could answer, Grandma Julie rushed in. "Jeremy, my dear boy!" I knew Jeremy was hoping she didn't reach for him under his armpits. "Don't monopolize my baby, Dwayne," she said to my grandpa. She was about to reach for Jeremy. I had to save him!

I stooped down to Jeremy's height and held his mouth open. "Look, Grandma, all Jeremy's teeth are grown back!" I exclaimed as she did the same.

"Ah, that's wonderful!" she said, examining Jeremy's mouth for herself. The moment passed and Jeremy survived yet another lift in the air.

Grandpa Dwayne greeted me as Dad grabbed his bags after a bear hug. "Hey, tyke, up to anything good these days?' He patted my head as he'd done Jeremy. No gender greeting differentiation, that one. "Not much," I said. "Great to see you!"

Jeremy offered the latest newest information. "Dad's going to be Saint Nick!"

Grandpa Dwayne replied jovially, "Oh yeah? Took away my job did he? Hah, that I gotta see."

We all went in laughing and happy. Christmas had begun.

SIX

Grandma Julie is the most amazing character you've ever seen. I've never seen less than five colors on her at any given time. Her nickname's Rainbow mostly used by Grandpa Dwayne so not sure if it's official. She also never goes out without a wide-brimmed hat. She's really short too, reaches Grandpa somewhere around the elbows.

It was Christmas Eve and she was making breakfast in the kitchen, singing Jingle Bells. "Bonjour, grand mere," I cut in, hoping to impress with the French I'd learned in class that week. My first class.

"Oh, my little frenchie, bonjour."

"Thanks, Grandma." I replied, hoping she was going to start speaking English again before too long.

"Coment savant…?"

"Huh?" I hadn't got that far in class.

She cracked up. "Didn't know your old grandma spoke French, did you?" (Well I was hoping she didn't, I thought).

"I had a blast in France in my early twenties before I hooked up with that old man in there," she said jokingly, tilting her head in Grandpa Dwayne' s direction. I'd walked past him and my dad in the family room playing cards. "I was going to be a famous artist, like Van Gogh, oh yes I was."

I always thought Grandma Julie's paintings were pretty. Mom had them hanging up all over our house. "My friend Jimmy says that most famous artists were gone long before they became famous. There's still time. Did you like Paris? It seems so far away.

"Not really dear. The world's a pretty small place when you consider how big the universe is. It took us only seven hours to get there. My closest friend from college and me. Her name was Jackie. We'd planned on being starving artists, sacrificing food for art. We spent our days painting on the streets of Paris near Champs-Elysees and selling our work to eat French bread, croissants and coffee, the French staple. Oh, and cheese, the French have the best cheese. All this talk of French food gives me an idea. I'll make you French toast for breakfast!" she said with a flourish. "You like French toast, honey?"

"I probably would, if someone had ever made it for me."

"Well, wait no longer. Grandma Julie's here."

Hopefully this would be her first success. My Grandma Julie's a lousy cook. I mean, who puts walnuts and cabbage in macaroni and cheese, then garnishes with sliced glazed cherries and calls it their macaroni and cheese special? Macaroni and cheese. Two ingredients. That's what makes it special. Jeremy the vegetarian was the only one who gobbled it up.

Grandma Julie continued, "When we weren't eating French bread and painting, we were practicing our French for when we returned home to tantalize the boys. They say French is the language of loooove. When I first met your grandpa Dwayne when we returned to America, and he asked me my name I replied in my best newly acquired French accent, Je m'appelle Julie. And he's been hooked ever since."

"No kidding, Grandma," I replied with my straightest face possible. She'd say jump, and he'd ask "How high?"

"Boy, it's hot in here," she said as she fanned herself with a potholder.

Grandpa Dwayne waltzed in, he must have guessed we were speaking about him. "What's going on in here, Rainbow? Sounds like a racket," he said, using his favorite phrase that cracked Jeremy and me up.

"You're the racket, Monsieur Kendall," chided my grandma.

"Oh, monsieur? Speaking French today madam? Nice, must be Christmas. I'm tingling jingle bells," he joked.

"Hush up, old man, and help us set the table for Christmas Eve breakfast!"

The French toast was burned almost to a crisp, but we all enjoyed licking the maple syrup we piled on.

"Come on, Carol. Get this one," yelled Ms. Rake, our dance instructor, exasperated with me. I can tell. Christmas vacation was now over and Grandpa Dwayne and Grandma Julie left yesterday. It seemed awfully quiet at home since.

We had a dance recital approaching. Ms. Rake was looking pretty nervous. We had to make her look good. Jimmy twirled me, and again I lost my balance, almost tumbling to the floor.

"Don't know what's wrong Ms. Rake but I'll get it!" I explained confidently, while mouthing over to Jimmy, "Work with me here."

"Should have taken it easy on the Christmas pies," he mouthed back. Truth be told I'd gained five pounds over Christmas and was tempted to stick my tongue out at him, but Ms. Rake did not tolerate what she considers infantile behavior.

"Are you calling me fat, skinny Jimmy?" I retorted back.

"Wouldn't dream of it, but boy, my arms are aching from that lift," he teased. I girl punched him on his right arm.

"Hey! Easy, dancer," he said, rubbing his arm and pretending to be hurt.

"Well, perhaps you should have had more pie and packed some muscle on those sticks."

"Would have, but seconds were scarce around my house these holidays. Financial troubles." I felt really ashamed. Jimmy had said last term that his parents were going through a tough patch financially. "Sorry, Jimmy. I didn't mean that. Did you guys have enough for Christmas? We could have brought you over some of ours."

"We did have enough, dancer. Thanks," he said with a smile. I could tell I was forgiven. "We skipped pie! Who needs it?"

I couldn't agree more as I was paying for it right now. Christmas pies and no dance classes for almost two weeks. That'd do it.

"I also have Bonnie's to look forward to," he glanced at his watch, "fifteen minutes," continued Jimmy.

"Are you guys humans or dancers over there?" barked Ms. Rake. That was our cue that chit-chat was annoying her, and we headed back to work.

"Dancers!" we all yelled back in unison.

Wonder if she'll be this tough on her dancer babies. They'll probably only be human for a day. The day they were born.

Ms. Rake was sporting a huge diamond ring. It looked too big to be real.

"That was grueling," complained Jimmy after class.

"Nothing ice cream can't fix!" concluded Brittany.

"Can't wait till we graduate and become human again. Ms. Rake is on the verge of ruining my love for dance. We need a new teacher."

"Did you see that rock of a ring?" I asked no one in particular.

"See? That thing was blinding me. Made all of my moves cloudy," agreed Jimmy comically.

"My mom says she's engaged," said Brittany. "It looks like she's finally snatched one up."

I now felt responsible for the gossip direction that this conversation was heading. "Hey guys, look! My mom's here," I announced. My mom arrived on cue to save me. The gossip police.

The following week our dance recital was a success. We got standing ovations and I truly felt human. Ms. Rake beamed almost brighter than her ring.

SEVEN

One evening after dinner, I felt my world crumble around me. My dad had made a startling announcement. "Why, Dad?" I asked, emotionally distraught. With a slight raise of eyebrows, he said, "You need to focus more on your studies. You are now in junior high, and this monthly discussion is no longer necessary."

"Not necessary to whom? To me it is!" I continued, pleading for his understanding.

"Come on, Carol, I must get to bed, I'll sleep on it," was his response.

"Okay," I replied. It looked hopeful. I guess that'd have to do for now. Maybe he'd have a dream.

Other than that one picture two years ago, I'd made no other find. I was convinced that my dad's mother was alive, but how could I find her in a big city like New York, with no other clues? Somehow, everyone was convinced she was dead. So finding her was totally up to me. It was my mission. If I told anyone what I was thinking, they'd take me to a mental institution and you've heard people go crazy in those.

I now attend St. Joseph's All Girls' School. Couldn't say I missed going to school with boys other than Jimmy who I still saw regularly at dance anyway. Plus my body was developing in all strange ways. I was even beginning to look like my mother. At last! Our wish for a new dance instructor had also come true. Her name was Jenny, and she was awesome!

45

"No need to call me Miss anything," she'd announced on our first day. "I'm just Jenny." Must be human, I was thinking. Sweet.

Sometimes I wondered if anyone suspected my ulterior motives for pursuing dance. For example, this out-of-the-blue question from Karen one day last week at Bonnie's.

"So, do you plan on being the best dancer ever?" she asked, eyeing me over a huge banana split that looks like it's about to topple over at any moment.

"Why?" The guilty are always on the defensive, of course.

"No reason."

"I thought that was your dream."

"Well, there's always room at the top for one more," she answered cockily.

"Don't count me out now," injected Brittany.

"…and a primo male," added Jimmy. By now the attention was off me. Whew. That was close. Always ask 'why' when you are put on the spot.

We all had decided on attending the same dance school in New York after graduation, and there was always talk of it, which suited my New York obsession fine. So that angle was always encouraged.

"My mom says I'll have to find a job once I get to New York and pay my own rent," said Jimmy.

"Our parents say food's covered. They won't see their only twin-born starve in the streets of New York City," said Karen. That's some consolation, I'm thinking.

"Well, at least that's something," I said instead. I couldn't help agreeing with such a noble parental decision.

"Dance is so draining. Working as well will be extra draining," I said.

"Well, it's either that or squash that dancing dream," declared Jimmy whimsically.

That really got me thinking. "Maybe we can write to Bill Gates. See if he'll sponsor you guys. He's got so much money and has been known to give some of that loot away. I mean, how could you not, with so much money coming out of your ears? Probably go straight to 'you know where', if you didn't. It'd be like playing afterlife Monopoly. 'Do not pass go. Go straight to…!'"

We were all cracking up at this point, albeit nervous laughter, not so certain of our own immortality for some reason. It's not like we'd ever done anything so bad.

The nervous laughter ended as my mom looked up. She'd been at the table beside ours, on her cell phone the whole time— no doubt with my Godmother Lady Hall —and had somehow caught a whiff of that last joke. My godmother was of part British noble ancestry but had migrated to America she said to find her true roots.

"Be concerned with your own afterlife Monopoly," she advised.

"Very, funny Mom," was my still somewhat nervous response.

"It's pretty unsettling. That it is, dear Miriam, and do stop all the fussing," Lady Hall insisted to Miriam. Miriam couldn't help herself any more than Lady Hall could. Fussing over each other was what they did.

Outside of God, her husband and her children, Miriam lived to serve Lady Hall. Lady Hall held some of the secrets, if not all, that would free her daughter from the dark nights to come. She thought that she was on her way to solving her grandma's mystery in New York City, but there was so much more she didn't know. Not even Miriam. Not even Lady Hall. Having chosen Lady Hall to be the godmother of her first-born was no coincidence. If indeed such a thing did exist as coincidence.

She'd heard a catch phrase once that said, 'A coincidence is simply God being anonymous.' She had met Lady Hall three months shy of her wedding to Marc. They'd run into one another in the cereal aisle of the supermarket. It just proved that she hung out there, as usual, a bit too long deciding on healthy or sugar. Cereal was Miriam's passion—something she and Lady Hall had in common. Miriam could live on the stuff (a long running joke in her home growing up) and quite literally had done at certain points in her college days.

"Can't make up your mind, dear?" said a thick voice with foreign accent, momentarily jerking Miriam out of her cereal day dreaming. The accent: British, Miriam thought. The voice no doubt belonged with the whiff of Chanel No.5 she'd gotten earlier, when she'd first entered aisle seven. Trying her best to ignore the person who'd invaded her cereal world, Miriam went right back to staring at the cereal boxes. The British accent wouldn't let up. Miriam was used to many tourists in Berkeley Springs from all over the world who visited for the mineral baths. Not that the British lady couldn't be a local but the town was so small Miriam thought she pretty much knew everyone. Something she actually enjoyed. She wouldn't live anywhere else. She'd convinced Marc to move to this small town shortly after they were married. They'd both graduated from West Virginia State University the same year. Marc had been quite happy not to move back to his old hometown in Wyoming, with all those awful memories of his late childhood years.

"I go through the same, dear. Don't feel weird or special. Thirty of my forty-five minutes grocery shopping is spent right here deciding between healthy or unhealthy. Sugar, they call it."

With that statement, Miriam couldn't help but turn around and smile at the voice, which happened to belong to a slender built, elegant woman with jet-black hair with hints of early grey. Miriam was guessing mid- to late forties.

"Hi," she said.

"Hi, I'm Lady Hall. Elizabeth Hall. My friends call me Liz."

"I'm Miriam."

"Difficult decision, isn't it?'

At that, they both burst into fits of laughter. "You must come over one afternoon and join me for tea and scones," said Lady Hall.

Tea and scones? Miriam was thinking. In Berkeley Springs? Sure, possible.

"Oh, thanks," replied Miriam, glancing at the business card the British woman had handed her. It read 'Time for Tea,' and captioned below: Put some class in your events.

At that, Lady Hall had made one last sweeping inventory of the shelves and chucked Cocoa Pebbles and Captain Crunch into her cart, and took off with one last whiff of Chanel No. 5. Miriam hesitated for about two seconds and proceeded to pick the same two boxes of cereal.

The next day, Miriam telephoned Lady Hall—although she'd never intended to do so. It was as if she was compelled. Two days after the phone call, she was having tea and scones at Lady Hall's manor, and soon thereafter a friendship developed. One month after meeting her, Miriam became Lady Hall's personal assistant. Miriam just happened to need a job, and Lady Hall an assistant.

After Miriam and Marc were married, seven years later Caroline was born. Lady Hall was chosen to be Carol's Godmother. Who else? In those seven years, despite an almost twenty-year age difference, Lady Hall had become Miriam's closest friend. Though their friendship and professional relationship did have their ups and downs, they were mostly ups.

"Miriam, dear, you're wandering," said Lady Hall, jerking Miriam back to the present. "You were miles away," she continued.

"You're right, Liz, but I'm here now. You know you enjoy me fussing," she replied.

"Whatever would give you such an insane idea, dear?"

"Oh, you know, the voices in my head, of course."

"The voices? Oh, Miriam, you are entertaining," said Lady Hall, pausing briefly and taking inventory of Miriam's weight. "My, you've lost weight. You could be blown away by the slightest wind," she continued, acting as though the matter of Miriam's weight was of most importance at the moment—which of course it wasn't.

"Come on, Liz, let's not get distracted here. "You said there was no other way, but there's got to be. "How do we know that she can handle what's ahead?" asked Miriam.

"We must remain calm, Miriam. I was put into this predicament the moment the child was placed into my arms at her baptism and those visions appeared. I wish there was another way, but there isn't, and do stop fussing over those pillows. I simply have the flu. I'm not bedridden."

"I know, I know," replied Miriam, continuing to prop up more pillows under Lady Hall's head. "I just wish there was something we could do. I feel so helpless."

"Don't underestimate the child, Miriam. It's her destiny. I've finally figured out why I was given those unsettling images at the church, but as you know, I don't have all the answers or know how all of this exactly is going to play out. But we must have faith. I wish I could tell you more," Lady Hall concluded wearily.

"Forgive me, Liz, but it just tears me apart not being able to share this with Marc, watching her go through all of this and making her plans to go to New York, knowing there's nothing I can do to stop her. Maybe if I'd discouraged her from dance?"

"You know it's futile. The powers that be have been controlling that child from your womb, and there's nothing that we can do. Her Grandma Lily needs Caroline to help free her, and that's all that matters to them—and to Caroline as well, for that matter." Lady Hall always preferred using Carol's full name. True, she loves us all dearly, but she is compelled to the matter of Grandma Lily. Marc will know at the appropriate time." Lady Hall took a sip of her lemon tea, which was now ice cold, and handed Miriam her cup. "Iced tea, dear, an American treat."

Miriam burst into tears and laughter at the same time. Lady Hall handed her a tissue, which was always at arm's length.

"Now you're your old self again! Sit down and rest, Miriam," she said. "You'll worry yourself sick, and that won't do Caroline any good whatsoever. She needs our strength and vigilance, and you know our part is most crucial to her success. If we become dysfunctional and lose faith, it will be her downfall."

EIGHT

"Carol, have you seen my red fire engine truck?"

"Can't say I have, Jeremy," I answered truthfully. "Been on Google all day."

"Well, seeing I have your attention, I was wondering when you were planning on leaving for that fancy school in New York?" Jeremy asked, giving me a piercing look.

"Can't wait to get rid of me, J? Need more space?" I had the bigger bedroom, of course. I'm older.

"Well, I do, but that wasn't why I was asking."

"Oh?" I was getting suspicious. I'd heard of kids with telepathic powers. Jeremy would be one of those.

"I was wondering because after you left, it'd be like I was an only kid and I wouldn't like that. Those kids are spoiled rotten."

"Not all of them. Ask mom and dad, they were only kids," I replied clearly amused and thinking I was off the hook and my secret was safe. I could drop my guard. "Come here, you." We exchanged a brief hug. Jeremy squirmed. Getting back to the business at hand, he continued, "Well, I can't risk it. Promise you'll call every week so Mom and Dad remember they have another child."

"Scout's honor. Anything else?"

"Yeah, why do you like dance so much, anyways?"

"You've seen me dance. Don't you like it?" I asked. I was hedging. Didn't think I was totally out in the clear just yet. New

York is the place for professional dancers and besides, it's fun there."

"We have fun right here. All the way to New York for fun?" he said, eyeing me quizzically.

That seemed almost too close to an 'I know what you're up to' kind of question. I counted my options and said nothing, staring at my Google page intently like it'd just been discovered.

"So?" persisted the kid from Mars.

"So…nothing wrong with having fun while pursuing bigger causes of becoming a famous dancer. Now I need to focus here," I said hurriedly, praying that the badgering stopped. I could feel a headache coming on, which had nothing to do with being on Google all day.

"Bigger causes, huh?"

"Yep."

"Well, keep your little secrets. Just don't forget our deal," he said, eyeing me sideways with his parting comment.

I seemed to be at a dead end with my Google research, anyhow. There were too many people in New York with our last name Brandt. I hadn't made any progress.

Sometimes I wondered what my dad would have been like as a little boy. Say, around Jeremy's age. Jeremy is now around the same age my dad was in that letter his mom had written to him, which I'd found. It must have been really hard for him. That had to be the reason he was so closed up and got that faraway look in his eyes at times, when he thought no one was paying attention, but I was. Sometimes Jeremy tried to act so grown up, but I knew he was just a little boy, just like my dad was at the time. I hoped to get some more clues before I left for New York. Was I just shooting in the dark? I didn't want to lose hope. I prayed for some answers.

That night, I had a dream. My blue monster friends had returned chattering and this time pointing to a meadow. And that's when I saw them, the couple and the little boy. The faces were blurry, but I knew it wasn't my family because the boy looked like he was all they had, and I am older than Jeremy. He was playing with a ball. There was a beautiful woman lying on the grass with a radiant smile, watching him. Her back was turned and I couldn't see her face. She had long hair just like my mother's. There was also a man who looked a lot like my father. It was all so uncanny. There was the brightest light everywhere. Suddenly, the woman turned around and seemed to be beckoning me to her. It was Grandma Lily! Just exactly like the photograph I'd found many years ago. She was saying some words, but her voice was very faint. What was she saying? I really wanted to hear. Then I heard it!

"I'll be waiting, Carol," she said.

I woke up in a sweat and didn't go back to sleep that night. There was nothing else, nada, not a dream, for the next couple of years. After sleeping on it that night, my dad and I had one more discussion and then he'd never resumed the stories, and I never resumed asking.

Prom night came. Bye-bye high school. Jimmy and I were prom dates. Brittany and Karen had Kobe and Jake. Jimmy told them to.

"Cool," I'd heard their reply when he'd told them. That was easy. Brittany and Karen had no time for boys. Dance was their lives. So they were quite happy Jimmy had taken care of it. The prom was lame, but we're dancers, so we had fun. We'd also had the best last years of dance. Our troupe had won all except one dance competition.

A couple months after graduation, Brittany, Karen and Jimmy went on to New York ahead of me. Bill Gates had sponsored all three of them. The amount of letters he must receive, an angel must have delivered the ones we'd written. I couldn't wait to join them in New York.

NEW YORK CITY

NINE

My parents drove me to the airport. True to her word, my Godmother Lady Hall had kept her word. Not that any of us had doubted she would. I'm just saying. I'd also graduated high school at seventeen—didn't see that coming. As you know, math was not my favorite subject. Although, in my last years of high school, somehow I had grown a genuine appreciation for learning and did a little more than scrape by with a 4.0 GPA at graduation. Crying for help from my teachers definitely helped, as baby Jeremy had taught me. With that said, Yahoo! I was free to go! I didn't get to say goodbye to my Godmother. My mom had me write a note. I thought perhaps she wasn't big on goodbyes, although my mom had said she was a little reclusive these days. She was still giving a lot of money away to her charities but I'm sure none was as grateful as I!

I could barely keep my excitement down. My dad looked even more pensive than usual—perhaps thinking of what I might get myself into in New York, no doubt. His hands were pretty tight around the steering wheel.

"Dad, you know you need not worry about me with the crazies," I said, hoping to lighten things up.

"True, but they're pretty special crazies in the big cities. Call if you ever notice someone or anything suspicious."

"What if it's a five-year-old staring at me, the country bumpkin? That would be a waste of a long-distance call. You guys need to save up for Jeremy's college right?"

"Don't worry about that, sweetie. Jeremy's fund is moving along quite well, since we didn't need to worry about yours."

"Oh, that's great dad," I answered, once again grateful to my Godmother.

My mom was awfully quiet on the drive. She'd been quiet for months. She seemed just lost in her thoughts. When I'd announced I would like to be a professional dancer and move to New York she didn't even blink, it'd been really puzzling. However, I welcomed all the support I could get and was thrilled.

"Sis, just make sure you do not forget our little promise," whispered Jeremy in my ear, as we all made our teary goodbyes at the airport. It sounded real close to being a threat. Or else?

This would be my first time in an airplane. American Airlines, first class. "Welcome to American Airlines," said the beautiful stewardess with honey-brown curls and a killer body. Bet she got called by guys every five minutes for water, pills or whatever.

"Thanks, Ms.," I replied back to her cheerfully. My first time flying and I was in first class. I never understood the fear of flying that some people have. Look at the birds in the sky—a plane was nothing but a big bird. When the plane took off, I could see my family down below, waving furiously as they became smaller and smaller. Yes, finally! I leaned back to enjoy the ride. I was so ready for my adventure.

After dinner—I slept like a lamb till I felt the bump that signified landing. At some point I must have put my seat in the upright position or no doubt Ms. Beautiful would have woken me.

Jimmy, Brittany and Karen were all waiting when I ran out to arrivals, along with someone who looked like a New York crazy to me. They had brought big grins and flowers (which looked like they were trying their hardest to stay alive for me).

"You're finally here!" yelled Karen, rushing to hug me, as well as thrusting the poor, almost-dead sunflowers against my chest. Jumping furiously and hugging simultaneously, we broke out in a jig. We are dancers, after all.

"It seemed like forever!" said Brittany excitedly. "We thought you'd never get here."

"I can tell from the flowers," I reply jokingly. Seconds later, I was quite ashamed at Jimmy's downtrodden face. I was quick to add, "Glad they decided to stick around for me. Thanks, guys!" I sniffed the dark brown center of one of them. Ouch—who sniffs sunflowers? Overboard. "I've missed you guys so much the past two weeks!" I said truthfully, breathing in the cold New York air. "Wow! We're all here now… sweet."

Jimmy moved forward to hug me, always weighing and biding his time. "It's great to see you Carol," he said quietly. "I've rolled out the red carpet." Then he comically motioned the rolling out of invisible carpet with his long arms.

"Meet our new friend, Greg from California. He's the addition to our team of dancing globe trotters. The boy can dance!" Brittany said.

"And he knows New York like his pocket!" Karen added.

Greg has purple and pink spiked hair, wore tight black leather pants, purple cowboy boots, and a black cowboy hat with a feather.

"Nice to meet you, Greg," I said to him with a straight face. In my mind I was thinking, what a getup. My friends must have been really broken into the crazy city by now, with Greg as their tour guide. Jimmy announced that Greg drove them to the airport to get me. We actually had a driving friend in New York. Cool. I'd thought no one drove here. Misguided information, clearly.

"I love your hair color," I said to Greg, being careful not to stare too obviously at the rest of him. Never saw anything like it. If I'd shown up one day like this for breakfast at home, I'd be begging Jeremy for some of his tofu. And missing school that day too—which would have been great actually, except for the tofu.

"So you're the Carol I've heard so many things about," he said. Despite all appearances, I'm thinking, 'oh, so gracious.' Dad must be definitely wrong about the big city crazies. I didn't even care at this point. My hearing had moved up to top notch when I'd heard of his New York MapQuest brain. I'd surely need Greg. I wasn't making any headway with Google whatsoever.

"All good, I hope," I replied. To which Greg gave no response for a beat, not even a nose twitch. Then he smiled crookedly, just like Elvis—and I got it. He was funny and crazy.

Cool! We all burst out laughing and huddled into Greg's SUV. It was purple. I saw a theme here.

❂❂❂

New York is as mysterious and mind-boggling as my father. My apartment sat on the 23rd floor of an apartment building next to Central Park. Coming from a small country town, nothing prepares you for this. A city that literally, never sleeps and folks who never seem to have a shortage of things to do. Not all good, unfortunately! Trust me. I've seen 42nd street at night, on Greg's little tour of the city a couple days after I arrived. However, I was still backing up the thought: if you can make it here, you can make it anywhere
Apparently the others had already experienced Greg's little night city tour as well. So they all had the tour again, since there's no way any of my friends would have let me go alone, of course. Duh... Greg could only be trusted so far.
"You've got to see the dirty side of the city."
"Why?" I asked him, quite interested in the answer. This had to be good.
"So you know where you really are," he said. That had been his reasoning. After that little tour, there was no doubt in my mind of my whereabouts.
Jimmy, Karen, Brittany, Greg and I hung out most of the time when we weren't at school. We all lived within walking distance of each other. The others also lived in high rises, so no one was jealous of one another's skyline, which of course is a useless emotion anyway. And if the elevator were to break down for a week—rephrase, for an hour—we'd all be finding that out in a hurry. I prayed the elevator never would go out. I was not climbing twenty three flights of stairs. They'd have to helicopter me to that high-rise studio.
Karen and Brittany were roommates. So were Jimmy and Greg. I was the loner (I had asked extremely nicely to my parents).

"So what do you make of the big city, Carol?" asked Jimmy one morning. He'd popped by my apartment and rang the bell for me to come down. We all usually hooked up before class. "Well, I'm seventeen and can't get into any weird clubs but I'm digging it," I replied jokingly. "Why'd you ask?" Somehow I felt a nudge to share with Jimmy my secret. I'd never felt that before. I guess I was getting tired of the secret and needed someone to share it with and Jimmy had become my best friend. Now that I'd reached my destination, I figured it was time.

"Oh just curious," Sometimes I feel like there's something you're not saying."

After that statement I knew it was time to tell.

"Jimmy, I have something to share with you," I said to him. He looked at me quizzically. "You know I have grown to love dance but I took it up a few years ago with an ulterior motive. I'm here to find my missing Grandma on my dad's side. Her name's Lily."

The silence was deafening. "Oh my gosh, Carol how long were you going to keep this a secret from me, from all of us?"

"Not long," I replied. "Just long enough for you to know that hitting weird dance clubs is not my focus. I need your help to probably go to dark alleys and dangerous places."

"Too many thriller movies, Carol,"

Will you help me?" I reply ignoring the last comment.

"Where do you start? What info have you gathered so far, Agatha?" I was guessing Agatha Christie.

"Funny ha-ha. I've had a few dreams."

"Dreams?"

"Yeah, dreams. She actually spoke to me in one."

"No way."

Was that sarcasm?

"Way, Jimmy. I'm serious."

"You hear her voice and everything?"

"You're catching on. Took a while, but you're with me?"

"'Kay, I get it… no need to be smart, Alec."

"Sorry, sensitive issue."

"So what did she say in the dreams? Don't creep me out," he said with a grin.

"She says that she's waiting. And the blue monsters..."
I didn't get to finish.
"The blue monsters?" he interjected,
"In my dreams, they say she's in New York."
"Credible source."
I shot him daggers.
"Okay catching on but where? This is a big city. Do you even have an idea what she looks like?"
"I found a picture in the basement some years ago when she was around twenty five and she looked exactly like it in my dream."
"Well she's probably three times that now." He said.
"Not quite around sixty five," I reply.
"Other than she's in New York and a dated photo, any other clues?"
"Well...no."
"Great."
I felt a bit downtrodden. Jimmy was really beginning to put a damper on things.
"You mean all this time? Dance and everything? You kept this a secret from your parents too?"
"I had to. They'd never have let me come here. As it is, my dad thinks I have some crazy obsession with her." I was pleading with Jimmy for understanding and support, seeing as he was the first to get in on my secret. "Jimmy, he's so sad all the time. Ever since I've known him, and it's because of her. I know it."
"How do you know for sure that she's alive?" asked Jimmy suspiciously. He seemed to be really getting into it now. Boys, bet he thinks he can solve my mystery.
"Well, a sixth sense," I replied guardedly. "My dad hasn't seen or heard anything from her since he was seven."
After what seemed like an eternity of silence, he said, "I'll help you find her. Now, let's hit Central Park. I could use some sightseeing before class."
I was probably going to have to find out something soon...some clues that led me somewhere, if Jimmy were to stick around to help me.
Brittany, Karen and Greg joined us in the park for our little fun time. That was real good right now, because I needed to get

my mind off the fact that I'd just shared my biggest secret. Though I felt like a big weight had been lifted off my chest, I still needed the distraction! We all had the same thing every time: Smoothies and health bars, the dancer's diet. Then we would sightsee. Sometimes we jogged.

Greg was wearing something really out there somewhere today. He said it was his creative side that he gets from his mother, whom I just have got to meet. It was a green sweater over a pink t-shirt, knee-high black leather boots, and a cowboy hat again. Really?

"Hi Greg," I said nonchalantly, like I didn't notice the garb.

"Hey, cookie, what's cooking?" he replied with his one-sided Elvis smile. I swear he could break out into 'Jailhouse Rock' any minute.

Chocolate chip, I'm thinking, should be my reply, but I said, "Nada much." I was picking up some kind of Spanish from the Puerto Rican New Yorkers already. "Jimmy and I are just waiting on you guys to show up, mi amigo," I replied as I continued with my newfound foreign language, which he ignored. Typical Greg.

I greet Karen and Brittany with our usual hugs.

"Cool Chiquita," said Greg. That got us going into fits of laughter.

"'Kay, clowns. Let's have our usual and a sightseeing jog," said Jimmy.

That was our last normal day.

Next day, I had word of my grandma's last whereabouts. The news came via Greg. He'd found out that my grandma may have worked in a nightclub down on 42nd street.

Coincidence? I think not. I had no idea how he'd come up with that information, but I was ecstatic! Jimmy and I had shared with Greg yesterday that I was on the hunt for my missing grandma. Since he knew the city like his pocket, he'd been our first choice of confidante. Good thinking. In less than twenty-four hours he had information. Gotta love this crazy! Seemed like his research had come up with a clue that lay in a wine cellar underneath the club that she'd worked at. Was it another coincidence when he'd brought me to see that shady part of town when I'd first got here?

We were on our way to class around 2 p.m. when he ran up to me with the astounding good news.

"Carol I've done some research for you and one of my people came up with a clue of a woman who had the same name as your grandma, who worked as a cocktail waitress at a nightclub called Club Monet on 42nd Street."

His people? Okay … "What? How did you find that out? Are you sure? You think it's her?" I asked excitedly, tugging at his purple sequin-clad arm.

"Easy, boy…new shirt."

"Come on, Greg, I'm serious!" I rushed on excitedly.

"I'm serious, too. New shirt," he said again, carefully brushing smooth the linen on the sleeve I'd come close to ripping. Can you believe it? At a moment like this? If he only knew, he wouldn't be so nonchalant about the whole thing. However, I couldn't show my annoyance. I was too grateful.

"Sorry."

"No problem, Chiquita. It's a shot. She'd be in her sixties now as well, and they said she spoke of a son that was taken from her."

"Wow! That's the first real clue. What a find. Thank you, Greg!" I said enthusiastically. I gave him a huge hug.

"The shirt, princess! You're ruining it."

"Sorry again, mi amigo. I have to go there now. Talk later, going to find Jimmy!"

"Be careful!" he shouted to my disappearing back.

"Don't worry!" I yelled back to him, racing to find Jimmy.

I found Jimmy in the locker rooms, getting ready to go into class.

"Jimmy, you won't believe it! Greg's found a clue of Grandma Lily. You must go with me to this club on 42nd Street!"

"Amazing!" said Jimmy, hugging me—but I couldn't stand still. This was groundbreaking news, and the closest I'd ever come to a breakthrough.

"We must hurry!" I continued excitedly. "I have a feeling I'm running out of time. Let's skip class!"

"Whoa, dancer, hold up. It's been thirty years. I hardly believe one hour more can make much difference."

"I won't be able to focus anyway. I'll probably mash your feet to pieces. I'm way too excited!"

"Really? Nothing I'm not used to. Come on, we'll leave after class and see if they're even open. Most clubs are only open at night, dancer."

I couldn't argue with him. I wasn't going to 42nd Street alone at night.

That was the longest hour of dance I'd ever lived through.

TEN

W e got off the New York subway and began to walk toward the Club Monet. It seemed like there were eyes watching us everywhere. I just thought it was paranoia on my part, since my big moment was affecting my nerves. I was excited, but I was also nervous. What would we find out, who should we talk to, and questions of that nature were running through my brain, needless to say.

We got there right around 5 p.m. The front door was closed but unlocked. When we walked in, the place was downright ugly and appalling. A really decrepit place which looked like it should've fallen apart a long time ago. I couldn't believe a place looking like this could still be in operation.

There was someone in. He had his back turned to us, cleaning up and mopping the floors, I think. When he heard the door open, he didn't even turn around. All he said was "Yes?"

"May we speak to you?" Jimmy asked him.

"Who would like to speak to me?"

"We would," Jimmy said matter-of-factly.

"What do you want from me?" the man replied.

It was a bit dark in the club, and since this guy had his back turned to us the whole time, we had no idea what he looked like, except for something skinny about six feet tall, topped by a mop of brown hair. He wore faded blue jeans and an old baseball cap, no shirt, and his back was scarred.

"Sir, we're really sorry to bother your work and interrupt your day, but we just need some information, if you could help us."

"Go ahead," he said, mopping even more furiously now.

"We are looking for information on my friend's grandma, who was last known as an employee here. Lily Brandt."

The moment the words left Jimmy's lips, the man's mop and pail went flying as he let out a loud shriek and turned to face us. His face was cut up really badly too, with scars all over it. That was painful to watch, but I didn't have to look at it for long.

"You must leave now! There's nothing I can tell you, except time is of the essence. Go downstairs to the wine cellar, now. Run!"

"Wait a minute. I know we need to go to the wine cellar, but first if you could tell us—" Jimmy started to say. Before he could finish that thought, we heard the gunshots at our feet.

He didn't have to tell us twice. We were heading to the wine cellar.

"Run, Carol, run faster!" Jimmy yelled out to me, clearly out of breath.

"I'm going as fast as I can, I swear!" I replied, dodging the bullets which seemed to be now flying over our heads. We ran in leaps and bounds over what seemed like an eternity to find the wine cellar, but where were the bullets coming from? There were no people in sight. We could still hear the gunshots from behind us .Then as quickly as the shots had started, they came to a standstill. Then all was quiet.

It was eerie. We realized that we had made it to the wine cellar. There must have been hundreds of bottles of wine. Suddenly the top floor above us opened and we could see the sky and all the bottles of wine disappeared and as if by magic Jimmy and I were catapulted into the air and rudely dumped onto a massive green field.

PART TWO

THE LAND OF POSSIBILITIES
DAY 1

ELEVEN

I was about to pass out. I couldn't believe what had just happened. The field had the greenest grass I'd ever seen and it encompassed miles and miles. It was extremely enchanting and above us in the sky, there was an amazing rainbow unlike any I'd ever seen. Before I could take all this beauty in suddenly out of nowhere flew this giant yellow bird. It was like none I'd seen before, not even in story books. The yellow was blinding. It had wings that spanned at least twenty feet, and had the face of a man. Let me say that again: the face of a man, and with human feet to match! How could that be?

I rubbed my eyes profusely and did a double take. Whoa! It looked like it was about to land on my head. No! Couldn't imagine a bird this size going to the bathroom on my head. We were in a state of shock and could barely move or see. Then it landed with a screeching halt in front of me, literally like that American Airlines plane I flew into New York on. The sound pierced my ears, and I could see Jimmy wincing. I'd lost all speaking ability. Believe me.

"Children!" it said in a voice that boomed like rolling thunder. Geez, it speaks in human tongue! Could it have been the one darting those flying bullets? Jimmy and I huddled together, holding our heads down, eyes closed. I was praying in high Latin it was about to say something other than, "You're right in time for my dinner."

We awaited the inevitable. "Children!" it boomed again. Man. The light was so blinding we were afraid to look up. I made no eye contact. "Children!" the thunderous bird boomed once again.

"YES!" we both screamed together. Jimmy was holding me so tight, I felt like I was about to break. His ribs were probably rattling away as well, no doubt.

"Well, now that I have your attention..." The bird's voice had lowered. That allowed us to raise our eyes a little. Then the blinding light dimmed a little. That's when I noticed the face. It was a kind face. I started breathing again.

"Do you know where you are?" it asked us, cocking its head to the side like birds do—the ones that don't talk, anyway.

"Huh?" I was completely incoherent of anything at this point.

"I said, do you know where you are?" it said, this time addressing Jimmy.

"Huh?" Same reply from Jimmy.

We were both in shock mode I'm thinking. Where in heaven's name were we? I wasn't quite sure if the kind face was a farce, and our life might depend on answering that question, so I took a go at it. "E--earth," I replied, my voice shaking... I had to give something a shot. "That's where we were a moment ago

The man-bird thing belted out thunderous laughter "Nice sarcasm, young lady, but that won't get you anywhere fast."

It seemed like it read my mind. Man! For the last couple months at home, 'Man' had been Jeremy's mantra. It was fast becoming mine—but that's just juvenile. I guess this was my stupefied speaking phase. No doubt man-bird had helped me along. My eyes lowered once again.

"Earth is very far away from here, young lady," it said.

I did a double-take, feeling faintish. "It's a dream, keep it together," a voice in my head said to me. I belted out furiously, "Wait a minute! I don't know who or what you are, but I have a family on Earth and we... -" I pointed to Jimmy. "Live in New York City." I took one step forward with hands on hips, a dancer's stance, and looked down. I meant up, at the giant bird-thing.

Jimmy tried to pull me back a step. He still hadn't found his voice. I turned to him. "Let go of me. This thing doesn't scare me!" Then back to bird-man, "What are you? You look like a bird and have the face of a man, and feet like Shaquille O'Neal. But you don't scare me!" I yelled with as much bravado as I could muster. As much to convince myself more than anything. Then with one move of a giant yellow wing, I flew straight up into the air. No, it didn't hit me. It just flapped a wing, and the sheer gust of the wind it blew had me flying up into the air. Then I landed with a resounding thud, straight on my behind. Ouch. Giving myself a nice rub, I get up.

"Don't say I didn't try to tell you so." Jimmy had found his voice. A bit late to save my rumpus. Timing was everything. I smirked at him.

"Listen!" it boomed again. "You now exist physically only in your mind. From now on, everything you do and everything you are is no longer of a physical nature, but all in your spirit…you have transcended as few have. The Possibilities are endless here… as it is also where you just left, though so few believe. You are in The Land of Possibilities!"

"What? Land of *what*?" I replied. "What are you, and how could I have conjured you up? You're nothing that I'd ever come up with in a million years. Wait, try a trillion."

"Listen!" it boomed again. It must have been talking to Jimmy this time, because I was the only one answering back, so clearly I was listening.

"Still talking to you, Carol." it said.

Oh boy, the giant bird had read my mind again. How could that be? Am I that transparent? "Jimmy's listening," it continued "That's why he's not talking. With that line and without our permission, I guess none was needed, he scooped us both up onto one wing and we took off like a rocket into the sky. Talk about flying in the clouds. When I was in the plane flying to New York I was looking out into the clouds around me, feeling like I was in them but now I was actually IN them! Freaky.

No sooner had we sailed through the sky, it landed… "You've just traveled a million miles in a minute." it said as we both scampered off a wing. We'd landed in a beautiful field of daisies. "Now I must leave you," it said quietly.

"Leave us? Are you out of your bird-brain?" I screamed.

"Yeah, what do you mean, leave us?" yelled Jimmy as well. I think he'd woken up out of his daze. He seemed to be back.

"I must leave you."

The giant bird looked sad—or was I imagining things? I wanted someone to wake me up if this was a dream.

I started to cry. I cried so hard, I thought I'd fallen asleep. That's usually what happened. No, I was still awake. How long had passed? I had no idea. By the looks of things, not much, man-bird was still here, patting the wing of his jet down my back, and the kind face looking at me, suddenly taking on the form of my mother's face. I reached to touch her, but like a flicker of lightning, she'd gone. It must have been a trick of my mind.

"You!" I screamed, pointing at him, clumsily getting to my feet. "Take us back, now! You have no right to do this to me and my friend. He's only here because he was trying to help me and he didn't want me to go into that dreadful club alone.

He turned to Jimmy, knocking me aside with his massive wing. Jimmy helped me up and gave him a bland look, shrugging his shoulders. If I didn't know better, I'd swear Jimmy had now got really calm and was no longer afraid. He was probably just still in shock.

"I will return," said the bird.

"Forgive me as I break out in a jig," I answered back.

It stared me down.

"Sorry, but when?" I asked him, really annoyed and almost ready to beg for our return.

"The time is irrelevant," he said.

"To whom?" I glanced around at the fields of green and daisies we were in. This is beautiful and all but I was on a mission to locate someone!"

"Remember when you were on your first plane ride and had that thought go through your mind about look at the birds in the sky, they neither toil nor—"

"Okay, enough with the quotes and reading my mind. Do you have a name... or species, for that matter?"

"Man calls me many things. You may call me Rufus."

"So man, other than us two quite recently, knows of you?"

"Even those who pretend not to... and you should know all about that, dear. You've pretended your way, all the way to the big city in search of your Grandma.

"I had no choice! No one believed my dreams so I had it all a secret."

"Yes I understand child, it was a very pure intention. No need to get all huffy and puffy.

Then as he turned to Jimmy said, "Son, you know the ropes."

"What?" I was bemused and shaking. "Jimmy? What does Jimmy know?" I asked.

"You'll soon find out. Have patience my dear." Then just as majestically as it had appeared, it took off with a great big flap of bright yellow wings and into the sky, this time with lightning. It then made a 360-degree spin and paused in midair like the little hummingbirds do, except it wasn't little. Just before vanishing, it had these parting words: "I'll be back!"

I got it. I must be watching 'Terminator.' Though I know I'm not.

"Spill it," I said with clenched teeth, facing Jimmy head-on. "What's going on? You understand what's happening here?" I could barely contain myself.

"Some of it but not all." was his detached reply. How could he be so calm?

"You looked as scared as I was when the bird with the man's face appeared. Then it seemed like you two knew each other," I vented at Jimmy.

"I must admit, I was taken aback. Never seen him appear as that before. It was glorious!"

"Before?" I purposely ignored the glorious part. I didn't want to admit that yet, though true. Jimmy bent down and began to draw something in a soil opening among the daisies.

"What are you drawing?"

"Take a look."

I looked down. What I saw almost blew me away. It was man bird's face on an actual body.

"You know something. You know him/it! Where are we, Jimmy?"

"He told you. We're in the Land of Possibilities."

"You've been here before?"

"Yes."

"Yes?"

"Uh-huh."

Now I'm totally lost.

"When?"

"When I was around 6 months old."

"Six months old? You remember when you were six months old?"

"Yep, and before then too," he said to me.

Okay, badgering Jimmy wasn't working right now. I would try another route. I'd just have to get to the juice.

"Jimmy, I get it. You have a secret and that's okay. I've had mine too, which I only shared with you a couple days ago. What I really would like to know is what we're doing here, and when do we go back? The others will soon know we're missing in action. If I don't call Jeremy in a week, he's going to freak out. My parents are going to call. That's if the guys in New York haven't called them by then, and your folks. They're sure to be in a panic! Does any of that bother you?"

Before he could give me any kind of answer, suddenly emerging out of nowhere was the sound of a galloping horse. I turned and there it was, charging at full speed toward us. It was white and also had wings. A unicorn? What next?

"Jump on!" yelled Jimmy as he flew himself onto the white horse with wings while it almost rode past us. I'd never been on a horse—or a man-bird either, for that matter—so how hard could this be?

Jimmy pulled me onto it. I rode half-dangling for quite a ways. Once we were onboard, that thing's feet didn't seem like it touched the ground for a minute, until it rudely dumped us off its back, shut its wings, and took off again up into the air at frightening speed.

"What was that?" I asked Jimmy, already guessing his answer.

"A unicorn…" he replied.

"I just rode on a unicorn"…I repeated, flabbergasted. I had to lie down.

"Have you seen it before?"

"Uh-huh," he replied again.

"The uh-huhs are getting old, Jimmy. Level with me. You said you'd help me find my grandmother when we were in New York City. We entered a club, and now I'm some Alice in Wonderland!

Taking in our new surroundings, I noticed that the unicorn had dropped us off near one of the beautiful rivers I'd seen from the sky. It was the cleanest clearest water I'd ever seen even.

"Come on, let's get a drink," said Jimmy. I looked down into the clear water and noticed little tiny white rocks on it. It was so beautiful and pure that I wanted to eat them. We both made cups with our hands and drank from the stream. The funny thing is, as I drank the water a few pebbles snuck in, and when I swallowed, they slid down my throat like marshmallows. They were the tastiest things I'd ever eaten.

"Wow these are good… must be some kind of fruit."

He nodded.

I looked at Jimmy suspiciously. "You seem quite at home, like you're used to drinking with your hands. If I didn't know different, I'd think you were born here."

"I was. I was born here, Carol. I left when I was six months old."

"You l-left?" Now I was stammering. "What gives? You mean your parents took you away?"

"No, I left and they followed."

"Asserting your independence at six months old?" I asked, taken aback by the latest Jimmy discoveries.

Jimmy managed to produce a wry smile. There was a hint of the former Jimmy returning.

My parents at home aren't my real parents, I was adopted by them. Someone brought me to them from here. "I had to leave. There was no other way to save them or your grandmother."

I was baffled. "Save her? Jimmy was exasperating the daylights out of me.

"What do you know about her?" I demanded.

"More than I can tell you but in time all will be revealed," was his guarded reply.

"Okay, Jimmy, while you play your little cat-and-mouse game, let's go back to my question before the unicorn charged in. What about when everyone discovers we're missing?"

"I took care of it. Brittany, Karen and Greg already know you'll be gone for a while. So they won't be reporting us missing. My folks won't be looking for me at all and your brother Jeremy won't know, because we'll be back before your once-a-week phone call. As I recall, you spoke to him yesterday."

This was good news, I thought, finally.

"And our check in dance tutor mom is out of town this week," Added Jimmy. Oh yeah, almost forgot her. I thought thankfully. She would have been hard to keep quiet. One of the dance teachers at our school was supposed to look in on us now and then as a kind of parent stand in, especially the seventeen-year-olds, like me. When my mom had made the announcement I had suddenly acquired selective hearing. Anyway she hadn't had any time to hamper my research as I'd found out!

"So we're only here for a few days?" I asked warily, wondering what in heaven we'd be doing in those days.

"Six, actually," was his reply. That should give us enough time. That's right, Carol. We're still with the same plan to rescue your Grandma Lily. Now, will you cooperate and trust me, please?"

EARTH: LADY HALL'S MANOR

TWELVE

G et a hold of yourself, Miriam. We always knew this was going to happen. For this reason she came into our lives "We are her guardians. Well more accurately I'm her guardian. You're her mother and we must follow the divine plan," said Lady Hall matter-of-factly, reaching for a cigarette as she stretched out like a Siamese on the ruby red velvet divan. Quite a spectacle today in a flowing red robe, thought Miriam. However, the mousy brown, tangled hair did look like it needed a wash. Mental note.

"It's true, Liz, yes but I still worry that she has not been prepared thoroughly. Even letting her go to New York, that big city! And to be chased like a common criminal by darting bullets! It must have scared the living sense out of her. She's always lived a protected life, our Carol. You know that."

"The girl will surprise you, Miriam. She's strong-willed, with a mind of her own. She's always been determined to find her father's mother. There was nothing you or Marc could have possibly done to stop her. Thinking all along that you two didn't know of it."

"I know, but how I wish there was some other way, and we could have spared her the pain," said Miriam.

"It's not for us to spare her. It is her pain, as you've had yours, and me mine. This pain is not supposed to break her. It's only going to help prepare her for the mission. Besides, we've got too much to get done in too little time for you to spend it worrying your pretty little head over things you can't control. I know I sound cold but you know I couldn't even bring myself to see her before she left for fear I'd break down Oh, my. I could use a cup of tea, child."

"Very well," Miriam said, resigning herself to that answer for now. "I'll be getting the tea. By the way, your hair does need a wash today."

As Miriam walked toward the kitchen, they heard a loud bang, as if a giant rock had hit the house. Then it began to shake violently. Miriam began swaying in the hallway, almost smashing against the marble tile floor, but she managed to save herself from the violent blow that would have been caused to her head. She heard Lady Hall shriek in her drawing room. Then the shaking stopped abruptly as it had started. Running back to Lady Hall, Miriam found her lying as if unconscious—or perhaps dead.

"Liz! Liz!" yelled Miriam frantically, shaking her shoulders.

Suddenly Lady Hall seemed to wake up, demonstrating that by the opening of one eye. "Oh dear, what happened?" she said, slowly sitting up. "Are you okay? I must have fainted. Thanks to that dreadful noise and shake. That fiend always does make a loud entrance. The children have just had their visitor from down under. Let's pray."

THE LAND OF POSSIBILITIES: DAY 2

THIRTEEN

Suddenly I heard the creepiest laugh in history. I spun around to see where it came from as I heard Jimmy say, "My, my, what took you so long? Thought you'd never show up," to the thing that had just appeared in front of us. What was that? Talk about ugly! It was shaped like a ball, an extremely gross looking ball with long limbs. It looked like a revolting octopus but with red, bulging eyes. It was green in color and as big as tall as a horse! It had about nine of these long limb extensions, and it was jumping like a jack rabbit. I momentarily froze in fear. Very soon afterwards as I was about to run away from it, I saw one of its limbs lash out at Jimmy's face. Jimmy was motionless. I was about to hurl myself at the monstrous thing, no longer fearing. I was furious, and about to take it on. I had no idea how, but—

Jimmy raised his hand to stop me. "He's not worth it, dancer. Trust me on this one." Jimmy, still on the grass, raised his head to the thing, looking at him dead on. When it saw me charge at him it turned around furiously.

After that, everything happened so fast—I was getting used to that—it made my head spin. Suddenly there was a bright white light that emanated from Jimmy like a beam and darted out of his side and hit the ugly looking green octopus thing straight in the middle. The dart threw it off the ground into a fast spin in mid-air. It writhed in pain and was blown up into tiny, little ugly pieces, and then as if in a whirlwind, was sucked into the ground. Man.

"He should have known better by now not to try and lay his filthy limbs on me. "Who is he Jimmy? Are you all right?" I asked hurriedly. "Your face is bruised. Let's wash it in the stream. Quickly!"

"No need," said Jimmy, as the red marks disappeared right before my eyes and his skin returned back to normal, as if it'd never been touched. This blew me away more than anything thus far—and I'd seen a lot in the last few hours. So that said something. Then Jimmy eyed me speculatively, no doubt trying to decipher my reaction. It didn't take long.

"Jimmy who, what are you?" I shouted. "Did you do that? What special powers do you possess that you've been keeping secret from us?" I held my head, backing away from this friend I thought I knew, trying to battle things out as he led me further along this huge mass of green.

"The same powers you have if you knew how to use them."

"You're saying that I could do what you just did?" I asked, baffled at the craziness I'm hearing.

"At some point… but it would take a lot of work on your part, dancer," said Jimmy.

"Anyway, now you've met him. That one, you must stay alert. He'll always plan to get to me first, but there may be times when you'll need to see him sneakily approach you."

"How will I know?"

"You'll know. Come on," was his reply. "Let's get some sleep. There's a big day ahead tomorrow."

"Where do we sleep?" I inquired somewhat stupidly.

"Dancer, we sleep right here, of course. Where were you thinking, the Hilton hotel?"

I lay on the grass and tried to get comfortable. It was soft, I must admit. I'd have no problem sleeping after the last few hours. It was warm, like the perfect temperature. No blanket needed. No lights to turn off, either. It was still bright as day as we both slept.

I woke to a bright orange-red sun in an amazingly blue sky with white clouds. Don't recall it getting dark. I could see Jimmy lying on his back with his arms folded behind his head, staring above at the sky. For a second I was completely stunned and couldn't comprehend what I was doing laying here on this grass.

Then it all came rushing back, the events of the last twenty-four hours? I moan. I had no idea how long it had been, either! I do not wear watches, but I was willing to kind of rethink that policy when I got back to Earth. Surprisingly, I was still not hungry or thirsty. "Jimmy!" I called out to him.

As he approached, from God knows where, I asked, "How many more days?"

"Well hi there, Sleeping Beauty. Sleep well?" was his response

"Yeah, how 'bout you?" I didn't wait for his answer. "How many more days Jimmy?"

"Hold up with the questions, dancer. Breathe."

"You breathe. It never got dark? What kind of place is this, where it didn't get dark? Is this summer in Alaska?"

"Come on, morning grouch, stretch. It never gets dark here."

"Never?"

"Never."

"How do you explain that?"

"Nothing to explain, that's just how it is," he said.

"So how do you know how many days have passed?"

Jimmy showed me a little sand hourglass in his pocket. Prehistoric. I had no idea he even had one of those. I'd never even seen one before except in photographs. Letting it go for now. I could use some stretches. My dancer body needed it— though my dancing days seemed like thousands of years ago.

So we did some stretches.

"Jimmy, why am I not hungry? Is there an explanation for that? I know I don't see any food in sight. I mean regular food, these marshmallows were tasty as a snack, but that's no reason not to be hungry, is it? That's not like me."

"I know. We only eat here for fun. We never get hungry. Let me know when you want to eat for fun. Then the food will be here."

For fun? Interesting. I must have a lot to learn about the Land of Possibilities.

"Go wash up. We've got a lot to do to find your grandmother and very little time to do it."

"As I was asking, how many more days Jimmy?"

"Four and a half more," he said.

I think I must have slept at least the other half of the five. I walked to the other side of the stream and washed up.

Meanwhile, there's a couple of meetings taking place over the 'land'...all to assist Carol with what's to come, though she doesn't know it.

Jimmy and I got done with washing up and had started walking down a little pathway near the stream. Jimmy claimed to have the area mapped out in his mind. He said he knew where my grandma was being held, and it was just a matter of time till I'd find her. I mean, okay. I understood that she'd been captured by some undesirable folks and was being held captive, but how did you explain all the other stuff so far? My friend Jimmy, that I'd known since he was a brat, seemed to belong to some otherworldly group of those with powers unfathomable. I mean, light beams dart from his body. He said he'd been born here and left when he was sixth months old ahead of his parents so someone must have brought him to Berkeley Springs. That still didn't explain much. My mind went wandering to the past twenty four hours. I'd taken the ride of my life on a huge bird with a face of a man and rode on a unicorn. I saw an ugly-looking giant like octopus blown up by light beams from Jimmy's body and disappear into the ground. I was supposedly in someplace other than Earth, where no one gets hungry or thirsty, and when I got back home no one was going to believe a word of it. Nice going. And they'd probably lock me up if I said a word. Even if—I mean *when* I bring my grandma home, she tried to back me up. They'd probably think she got brainwashed by me on the ride home.

I began to eventually see some trees in the distance, looked like red oak or cedar, and a clearing as well—and then we saw them. There was a group of around seven, singing. Looked like all women, wearing pink and white flowing robes with pink roses in their hair. All looked young, not past sixteen, I'd say. So I knew my grandma couldn't be one of them.

When they saw Jimmy approaching, they started to bow to Jimmy (what in the world)? And speaking some funny language that still sounded like singing. I didn't get a word of it, but it was eerily beautiful sounding. Almost like I'd heard it before, but where? Déjà vu. However, I'm getting sidetracked. What is this? I was thinking. People are bowing to him, now? It couldn't possibly be to me.

I was right. They were also waving something made out of leaves, heralding his presence. Hail Jimmy?

We moved closer. Jimmy replied very politely to them. No way! He was speaking back in their language and translating to me. "They say they've missed seeing me and are happy I'm back, and they are welcoming you to join them in their group festivities this day."

"Oh—" I began to say.

Before I could say more, though I didn't have a clue what that would be, one of the women came toward me, smiling, and took me by the hand. Her hand was very soft and tiny. The other six beckoned to me to join them and not be shy. I gathered all that from sign language. They clearly realized I didn't understand "the language of The Land of Possibilities."

I hesitated, but Jimmy gave me a push. Their faces were amazing up close. They seemed to radiate light. I wasn't sure how old they were. The wise look in their eyes seemed as old as time, yet their faces looked as smooth as butter.

They formed a circle and sat me on the grass with them. They requested I join hands with them, and continued to sing in the most beautiful voices I'd ever heard. It was like angels singing. Not that I've ever heard angels sing, of course. I just thought that's what they'd sound like. These voices could send me right back to sleep again.

Then they got up and started to dance. I thought classical dance was beautiful but this was ethereal! I turned to Jimmy to help me out. I gathered this dance was in our honor? They ask me to join in using sign language. I shook my head, waved my hands, all the signs for I'll pass, but they wouldn't hear of it. I only wanted to be a spectator at this point. They'd probably laugh at what I'd learned at school as great as it was to earth — though they'd be polite, I had the feeling.

They pulled me by the hand, giggling, and I dared demonstrate what I'd been learning. They didn't laugh—not surprising. I was leaning toward their politeness. Bingo! Still, it was somewhat humbling. Suddenly I felt like I was flying. I wasn't dancing any more, for sure! My body seemed to be as light as air. I'd never felt this way in dance, ever, and wondered if I ever would again.

We were flying! All eight of us! We'd joined hands again in a circle, this time with our arms and legs outstretched way up in the air. I was awake too, I think. I felt goofy in my jeans and t-shirt, with their beautiful pink and white girly robes flapping in the wind but my t-shirt was flapping too, so I was cool with that. We were still singing as well—me too, this time. I was singing in their tongue? Unbelievable! I must have made a wish to at least sing in the language of the land because I could not recognize my voice.

Suddenly I saw Jimmy standing above us in the air, looking down and smiling. That's when I tumbled to the ground and blacked out.

"Master, do you think she's strong enough to handle what's coming?" I was seeing stars, but at least I could still hear. Master? Maybe I was watching a rerun of 'I Dream of Jeannie.' Before that, there'd been beautiful singing that I vaguely remembered before everything had gone dark. There were no genies that I recall, just seven flying ethereal beings in robes.

"I'm hoping she is. I'm counting on it," Jimmy said to Humility as he turned to address her. He'd been bent over me for the past ten minutes, singing. "You guys are doing an awful lot to help. I appreciate all of it. We do need to have her fully armored for what's ahead in two days. It's going to be rough on her down there. At least we know she can speak and understand the language now."

Okay, not 'I Dream of Jeannie,' but I couldn't seem to wake up. Jimmy was having a conversation about me to the ageless girls I was flying with earlier. The knowledge that I now speak the language of the land was clear. Their voices were fading again...maybe they'd drugged me. I tried my hardest to wake up, but I heard no more.

Jimmy drifted off in his thoughts, contemplating the past couple of days. It had been quite a lot for Carol to take in. Her world as she knew it was being turned upside down. He had to give her credit, though. As feisty as she was, she seemed to be hanging in there quite well, despite all the circumstances and newness of it all. From the run through the club with the flying bullets, she'd been so brave. Although he'd let nothing happen to her, she wouldn't have known that. She couldn't have. It was for this reason he'd been born. To protect her, to protect them all. Sure, he'd been a brat kid, but that was only camouflage. It didn't make sense to him, either.

"Master...?" said Generosity, interrupting his thoughts. "What more can we do to help? She'll soon wake up. Should we still be here? She could think it was all a dream if we're gone, don't you think?"

"Yes, but it wouldn't be true, Generosity. She needs to understand that this is all real. We'll all remain here together and go into the city when she wakes. You all get a little rest as well. I'm thinking of a five-minute catnap." He winked at them. They got it. They got him.

Returning to his previous thoughts as the others rested, Jimmy turned to look at Carol with admiration and joy. "Quite a noble undertaking for a young girl to have," he thought. "Such faith and courage to seek and find someone lost, solely to bring happiness to another." Frankly, she'd had no prior understanding of what finding the person would entail, and the frightening events that would occur. Probably thinking about some research in New York and knocking on some doors, but this? This was more than she could have ever imagined. Father had his way, though, and which he had to agree always played out quite nicely and some sense of humor that many didn't get. Carol luckily for her got some of it and didn't always take all of life too seriously.

He couldn't wait to witness Carol's reaction to the city. It would be the best time she'd ever been privileged to have. She might not want to leave, but work had to be done and very little time was left to accomplish her mission. Time meant nothing to him, of course—but for her lessons, it meant everything. That was all that mattered. This was his plight as well as hers.

The seraphs were great, as always. They were right where they were supposed to be, and had executed Rufus's wishes perfectly. The others were waiting in the city. She had to have some notion of what he was by now. It was all of their decision for him to appear above her like that in the sky. Whenever that occurred, it was always the right time and reason. Her passing out was just so she could assimilate all that had happened so far, and wake up with a more aligned spirit. He needed to have her spirit aligned with his before she entered underground. This rescue was her mission. To simply protect her was his. Rufus had given specific instructions on how it was all to play out. Not one thing could stop it. *Yet*, all the cards had to be dealt just right.

"Master, she's waking," whispered Patience. Carol was stretching like a Siamese and had opened one eye. The seraphs never really slept—that's why the catnap comment had been funny—so they had noticed Carol's awakening while Jimmy had been lost in his thoughts. He turned to look at her apprehensively. Yes, by golly, she was waking. He had to be ready.

"Is that you, Jimmy?" She reached out to touch his face gently, obviously still in and out.

"Yes, it's me, dancer. I'm here. You took a high fall."

It all came rushing back in loads. "No kidding!" she exclaimed, jumping to her feet. She was fully awake now. Carol got up, started pacing, and pointed at the seraphs. "I was flying with you girls...fairies...butterflies...I dare not say angels. I don't know what you are. Yes, I was flying!"

"I believe you've met," replied Jimmy motioning to the flying girls. "Humility, Generosity, Patience, Temperance, Diligence, Chastity and Charity."

The seraphs all giggled in unison, nodding their heads while still singing.

Ok, I get it a reminder for me to practice the seven virtues. I must have been lax in at least a few. I could think of one right now. 'Temperance.' Needed a lot of work.

"You're always singing." I say to them accusingly as if it was a crime? Then turning my attention to Jimmy, my temperance reminder clearly hadn't kicked in but my memory had.

"That's insane! Jimmy, what were you doing standing on air above us? I must be-am I losing my mind? I need some answers. I beg you for some answers, Jimmy, and I also clearly understand their language, I heard you and the flying girls speaking while I was asleep." I pounded, clearly past frustrated. "You're my dearest, trusted friend. Who or what are those flying, non-stop singing women and where are we? How long have I been asleep? I want out of here!"

Doesn't seem like the spirit is fully aligned yet—still work to do, Jimmy thought. "Easy dancer, you've just awoken and still a bit out of it, unable to assimilate it all, but you are making progress. You now understand the second language of the land that some speak, you still want to accomplish your mission, and you're going to and yes, you were flying. Isn't that wonderful? Don't question everything…enjoy it! We're about to go into the city, and you will see and hear things that will blow you away. You will pinch yourself every five seconds to see if you're still alive."

"I've got news for you Jimmy! I'm pinching myself right now!"

The girls giggled at that one. "Master, she's funny," they said in unison. Clearly timing was everything in this place.

Okay, I was beginning to really like them. But… "Jimmy. What's with the master talk and bowing to you? Are you some kind of royalty here?"

"You ask, or you say so?"

I couldn't help but make the association. The same response had come from the man-bird when I'd asked if he was God.

FOURTEEN

It looked like there would be no time to answer that question. No sooner had those words to me, escaped Jimmy's mouth, that I heard the sound of furious galloping heading toward us. I was thinking, unicorns. You?

Yes, I was right! More unicorns. Only this time they were approaching us at an even more alarming speed than previously. It looked like there were at least about a dozen. No doubt we could each have our own. I wasn't particularly digging that thought, since no one had given me a lesson thus far on how to ride a unicorn alone.

"Get ready!" yelled Jimmy above the galloping noise. They must've been getting closer. "We all ride our own unicorn," he said.

"What?" I yelled back. I heard but not comprehending. "I don't know how to ride it!"

"You will learn!" he yelled back. The girls were still singing. I must say it was soothing in times like this. They looked unconcerned. Something told me they rode unicorns often. Why? They could fly themselves! It must be for the thrill.

"I may learn but will I live to tell the story?" I said to him.

What a sight, as they approached us. They weren't messing around. They were in a hurry. A plane to catch? Didn't think so! I wondered if they'd stop this time. As if reading my thoughts, they came to an abrupt halt in front of us. I could have sworn the one that stopped in front of me was smiling, as if to say, "Didn't think I would?"

Jimmy was right. No sooner had I mounted the unicorn and took hold of its reins—I mean the fur around its head, since there were no reins—then I began feeling I was born to ride unicorns. Which I knew was completely absurd.

We started galloping, all nine of us. Must have made a majestic sight! Wish I had a camera, but who'd take the picture? It seemed like there were about three extra unicorns riding with us. Backup, in case there were more of us? Or perhaps they'd come along for the gallop. We were traveling at lightning speed. We must have been galloping just a few minutes when they took up off the ground, and we were flying!

I know I'm beginning to sound redundant about the flying, but I mean a lot of flying goes on in this land.

No sooner had we taken off flying than I began to see the city in the distance. I mean, it was huge. And I could see it all at once. It wasn't so much a city as it was a forest but there was magnificent foliage everywhere. Trees of every shape and size and they were so tall! It was breathtaking. I know I hadn't travelled much but I've seen many picture books and nothing that looked as beautiful as that. There were still rolling hills of green, but the green was magnified. If you've ever seen an emerald under shining light, you'd have a glimpse of what I mean. I haven't, but you get the picture?

However, amid this eye-catching green color was every color of the rainbow intertwined, shimmering like morning dew drops on leaves. It was so mind-blowing. If I didn't have a firm grip of the unicorn's fur around its neck, I'd definitely fall off— what am I talking about? I have absolutely nothing to do with my balance on a flying horse. Just one more thing this land could take credit for. I could see a glimpse of waterfalls all over the place that put Niagara Falls to shame. We also flew over lakes and rivers that shimmered like snowflakes. Enclosing it all, there was a coastline of delectable beaches surrounding it on all sides.

To herald our descent the unicorns let out a unified, braying bellow. They landed us smack down in front of a tiny gate and took off. At this point, I could see no more of the city—just this little golden iron gate. It was obvious we were going in single file. The unicorns had taken off as quickly as ever. I glanced around, and they were nowhere in sight. They were off with a neigh. Perhaps to pick up some more jolly folks like me? Those guys were always in a huge hurry and I must admit I was developing an affinity to those flying horses. I believe I'd truly bonded with my last ride.

I expected Jimmy, who'd been spearheading this expedition, to go in first. I saw no sign of a doorbell. However, the gate seemed locked from where I stood. I couldn't help but take a few moments to ponder for a moment on the divine picture Jimmy had made earlier, leading our way on the unicorns. He'd been something to look at! He'd looked so powerful and regal. It was very hard to recall the former Jimmy of...

Astonishingly, Jimmy said to me, "Go in ahead of us all, dancer. We'll be a couple of steps behind you." The girls nodded their heads in agreement. Looked like I had no say—I was outnumbered.

If I no longer mention their singing from here on, just know it was now a part of me. I no longer noticed. It's like living next to a freeway—I've heard that sooner or later you no longer hear or notice the traffic when hanging out in your living room, until a visiting guest says something.

I approached the gate and prepared to say abracadabra. No need. It automatically opened, and I heard a voice say, "Welcome! Carol!" I jumped out of my skin, clearly startled. I believe I'd heard the voice before. Déjà vu was really becoming a natural thing to me. What gives? They were expecting me? Where had I heard this voice before? I took a breath to calm and steady myself. I really had no idea what was expected of me. I needn't have worried. I was then given specific instructions by the now more-than-familiar voice that had read my thoughts. "There is no room for worry in The Land of Possibilities." It boomed.

The moment we got through the gate, it opened onto the wide expanse of green I'd seen from the air and now up close were also flowers of every color and variety and beautiful castle like homes made of pure crystal! The Berkeley Castle at home couldn't light a candle next to these. And the people were so beautiful and all looked so happy. They were either sniffing the flowers, singing, dancing, or laying out on the grass. They didn't seem to be concerned about anything but hanging out. If I were more metaphysical, I'd say they were simply being.

All the children were playing games and running around, and the parents were simply watching them, smiling. Everyone seemed to ignore us, or at least me. It's like we were invisible. That felt weird. I said hi to a little girl, and she kept right on walking. I tried again, said hi to a lady who seemed to be staring right at me, and she continued to speak to her son—or at least some little boy.

They couldn't see me! They could see Jimmy and the seven singing flying girls though, because they answered back to them when they said hi. One thing that stood out was that their faces were filled with light. I'd never seen anything like it.

Why was I invisible, though, and where were we going? I wondered. However, I was getting tired of asking Jimmy questions. His answers were always "wait and see," anyway. Pointless. I'd just enjoy being invisible. It's not every day that happens.

I also noticed many animals. There were lions, tigers, giraffes, dogs, cats, chickens and they all seemed to be playing with each other! Wow! They also ignored me.

"We'll be heading to that mansion over there," Jimmy said, pointing to what clearly looked like the biggest and brightest of all the castles like straight out of a fairytale. "We will have dinner with friends there, and spend the night."

"Yes, master," said the girls. I failed to respond. No questions or comments.

He eyed me speculatively. "So what do you think?" asked Jimmy, glancing my way.

"Just enjoying the moment, taking it all in," I replied. "It's not like you'll be giving me straight answers anyway, 'master'…" I said, throwing my hair back and walking briskly away from him as if on a mission, toward the castle.

As I'd mentioned all the mansions looked like castles, but what distinguished the one we were heading to, was the light that shone and bounced off its walls. When we approached the castle, there was no door. We walked right in. In fact, it had an in-and-out feeling, almost like it was a completely open house without doors, other than the roof and the walls which divided a few rooms.

As we walked in, the voice from the gate said, "We've been expecting you, Carol!" I now definitely knew the voice! It was Rufus's of course. But I couldn't see him anywhere. Instead, there was a beautiful table laid out with some of the most delicious food I'd ever seen, and lots and lots of fruit. I didn't know if I could eat any of it. I still hadn't been hungry or thirsty for two days. There was a pink card on the table that said: "In Carol's honor." Really? Cool.

"It's been a while since you've had a change of clothes," the man-bird voice said loudly.

I'm thinking 'if you'd been the one on the run…' but before I could finish that thought, I was suddenly clothed in this beautiful blue, flowing robe and matching slippers. So were Jimmy and the other girls—we were all dressed in blue. It also felt like I'd been given a shower. I touched my head, and my hair was wet.

"Now eat and be merry, Children!" the voice said.

I was still on my no-questions-asked policy, which had Jimmy stunned. I could tell from his face. He was highly misguided if he thought I hadn't noticed his enquiring, puzzled glances.

We all sat down to eat.

"Don't forget grace," said a most pleasant-sounding female voice this time. That voice I did not recognize. Rufus's wife maybe? The girls bowed to Jimmy. I ignored them and him and led grace. I usually was the one who led grace at home. I'd had plenty of practice. I could not mess up.

We then feasted on grapes, dates, berries, olives, little delectable finger foods and pastries that could only have been baked in a castle, bread that melted like butter on my tongue, the tastiest dishes that I could not tell you what they contained, even if I tried! I mean, man. I have no idea how I did it, because I clearly wasn't hungry, but I enjoyed this food like I'd never enjoyed food before.

Jimmy was holding an entire vine of grapes up to his mouth though eating them slowly one grape at a time. He looked like he was in grape heaven. I didn't even ask about the friends Jimmy had mentioned that we were supposed to be having dinner with, but somehow Jimmy read my mind again. He gave me an enigmatic, knowing look. I decided not to blink or look away.

"They're here. They're everywhere… all around us," he said, looking at me with those kind eyes. "That's why you were invisible earlier, so you'd believe that it could be possible. Our hosts prefer to be invisible as well, so we can enjoy ourselves together and not be shy or intimidated by their physical presence. It's their gift to you."

Marvelous! That's alright with me, I mused silently.

We ate, we danced and we sang songs. Gosh, we were merry! Right up to the point I went to sleep in one of the softest beds you could dream of. It was like sleeping on a cloud. I was used to sleeping in bright light now. There must have been a dozen or more beautiful bedrooms in just that one section of the castle. My room was oval-shaped, and everything was blue. Someone put covers over me, but it wasn't Jimmy or one of the flying girls. I couldn't see anyone there. I was getting used to all sorts of beautiful happenings in this land.

THE VALLEY OF THE DESTITUTE

FIFTEEN

Next moment I woke up in complete darkness. I mean the kind of pitch darkness that would scare the daylights out of you. I let out a loud scream. Where was everybody? What seemed to be moments before, I was eating the best fruit, and the most delicious bread and pastries, not to mention sipping divine fruit juices. Where was I? No doubt, no longer in The Land of Possibilities. "Jimmy!" I yelled out in fear and dread.

There was no answer forthcoming. Where were the flying singing girls? I'd thought we'd become fast friends.

A creepy voice said, "Welcome." This time it didn't address me by name, and it wasn't the man-bird's voice, either. I loved that voice.

This new voice almost seemed to say: we don't know who comes in here and we don't care. As long as you are here, you are welcomed. This voice sounded scratchy and evil, like in a horror film, except I wasn't watching television.

"Eeew!" I shrieked. I could feel slimy things that felt like fingers grazing my arm. "No, please don't touch me," I cried out. I still couldn't see a thing. I tried to run, but I couldn't move. It seemed like I was crushed into a tiny space. I could hear creepy sounds, like moaning, as if in pain.

I held my head and tried to pray. All I could say was, "Please, God, help me. Take me out of here." Almost instantly, I saw a tiny, flickering light. Not seeing was probably a better deal all round. What I got to see in this little light was terrifying.

What looked like thousands of bodies, were crouched together, writhing in pain, stretching out over long distances.

The ones up close, I could see their eyes. They were glassy. Though their bodies looked normal, they seemed to have no control of their movements. They all seemed to be asking me to help them. "Help usss," I heard one of them say.

I was moved, but I couldn't help thinking: Better chance I will if you don't try to touch me again. I won't pass out.

I wouldn't have wished this experience on anyone. Their arms were ice cold. Though it was terribly hot down here, I was sweating profusely. What a contrast. It made no sense, but nothing has lately.

"Where were Jimmy and the girls? How could they have abandoned me and let me come here on my own?" Guiltily, I began to think, what if something happened to them too? I hoped they were okay. How did I even end up here? When I fell asleep I was in The Land of Possibilities. Things seemed pretty bleak in this new place, not to mention desolate. How do I get out of here? And where was I? Was I dreaming again? Another dream. Is any of this real? Could I find my grandma already and get back to New York? In the flickering light I also then noticed I was back in my former clothing. My old jeans, t-shirt and sneakers. I remembered the beautiful silk robe and slippers I was just in. It was like a dream.

Suddenly out of the dark, I felt something move near my feet. Really slimy! I was catapulted into running. I'd suddenly found my feet! Then I heard the laugh. I remembered that laugh.

Something reached for the back of my neck and I felt its sting. I cringed. I could feel blood dripping down my neck. I continued to run in the dark, with just that little beam of light to guide me. I had a feeling that thing behind me wanted me. I ran past other slimy bodies that the moaning sounds were coming from. I could still hear the creepy noises. I must've been in some kind of tunnel, because the walls were closing in.

As I ran, the cold fingers still tried to reach for me from both sides, still crying. "Help us…" I would've loved to help them, but I'm afraid I was too terrified to help anyone but myself at the moment and what could I possibly do? Then all of a sudden I came to a screeching halt just in time. I must have done a Road Runner move there.

I was at a cliff. The precipice looked like a long way down. The tunnel had come to an end. Great! How did I get to the other side? I could still hear the running steps and evil laughter at my heels. I thought that thing that attempted to strangle me earlier wanted to complete its mission. What should I do?

"Jump!" said one of the creepy voices that I wished I could have helped. Wonderful, they must be on my side. They had also said run. I hesitated for a moment. My legs were not long enough to make it over that cliff. No way!

The footsteps were getting even closer. So close that although it was dark I could almost feel its breath. Out of time...I jumped!

It seemed I was transported over the deep crevice by some divine power. I looked behind me to see if Frankenstein had caught up with me. It was brighter now. I turned to see if it was who I'd thought it was. I guessed correctly. It was the same creature that Jimmy's light beam had pierced a couple days ago and had disappeared into the ground. The ugly, giant octopus thing. He must have missed me by a hair. Talk about a narrow escape. Whew!

Oh no, he looked like he was about to jump too. I picked up my heels without looking back. Then I heard the explosion—and turned around to once again witness Mr. Octopus blown up in pieces and again being sucked into the ground. He must be used to that by now, I was thinking. I felt the back of my neck. The blood was gone. Jimmy?

Before I could enjoy and bask in my amazing getaway, I rubbed my eyes in disbelief. I had jumped over the cliff and landed into the land of them. Yes, I was surrounded by hundreds of Mr. Octopuses. Yikes! I blinked and blinked again. No joke. However, glancing down, I noticed I was surrounded by a circle of light on the ground, like when I was dancing on stage. For some reason unbeknownst to me, it made me feel safe. I decided to stay put. No guarantee it would follow me around though. This was not a stage but for some reason the light scared them and all they could do is stare and move around the light.

"Well, well, what do we have here? If it isn't Lily's dear granddaughter," one of the things said as it moved closer toward the ball of light. It let out a shriek of pain when it almost touched it. Cool.

Then I heard a voice from behind me that threw me for a loop. "Carol, don't be afraid. It's me, your Grandma Lily. I always knew you'd come." A hand touched me from behind.

❀❀❀

Whoa. Talk about being startled! I spun around like a flying trapeze. "Grandma Lily? Is that you?" I was beside myself with joy! The moment I'd been waiting for, for the past twelve years, was finally here—but I couldn't really see a face. Everything was so dark and blurry beyond my ball of light. So far just a voice, but I could have sworn someone touched me. "Grandma Lily, Grandma Lily, I'm here! You must know I'm here. You just called out to me. Why can't I see you? I just heard you call my name! Where are you?" I called out to the dark, reminding me of some scary movie I'd yet to see. The silence was entirely creepy.

Then suddenly out in the distance, I heard a familiar voice speak. Oh my, it's...I couldn't believe it, but at this point I should've been beyond surprises, right? Not.

"Lily, speak to the child," the voice said. "You know she can help you. Don't be frightened, for Pete's sake. She's your key to unlatch the chains to be free! It's all she's ever wanted. It's what you've been waiting—hoping for," she said.

"Godmother, is that you?" I yelled out, completely flabbergasted and taken aback to hear a familiar voice from home. I must be going nuts and hearing voices. I felt so lost and all alone, and I was very close to tears now. "Can you hear me?" I cried out. "Is my mother with you? Where are you? I need to get out of here, you guys! Some very weird things have been happening since I got to New York. Jimmy was here, now he's no longer around and I am alone in this creepy tunnel. Jimmy has some strange powers, and how about you Lady Hall? How come—well, anyway, I think I've found my father's mother and she's being held captive. I must be going out of my mind. How can I hear you and not see you? I need my mother. Can you hear me Godmother? Do you know what's been happening?" I rattled on, so happy to hear a familiar voice, real or not.

"Yes, Carol, it is me, your godmother. Oh, where are my glasses? They're never around when I need them. Carol, I am communicating to you via another dimension, which I'm still at home in Berkeley Springs. Please stay calm. There is much you don't know, but you are veiled with a great amount of protection. Nevertheless, you must not take any of it for granted! Your poor mother Miriam and I are saying many prayers, and I'm doing my best to keep her calm. Not an easy feat, mind you—"

"Godmother I am surrounded by some monstrous beings at the moment!" I interrupted, tearfully as well as clearly frustrated. "I heard you speak to my Grandma? How is it that I can hear you and not see you and where am I? How'd you and my mother find me? This is so weird. Please help get me out of here!"

"All right child, let me speak. We understand your fear and we love you very much. Your mother doesn't get the whole picture as I do. She is really trying to hold herself together. She's praying the Holy Rosary non-stop for you and asking for Our Blessed Mother's intercession. We are communicating from home as I mentioned through another dimension—"

"Carol darling, it's mom, can you hear me?" interjected Miriam.

"Yes mom, I can!" I answered thankfully.

"We are doing all we can to help you darling. We are praying very hard," said my mother half tearfully trying her best, I could tell to sound strong.

"Mom I am so afraid," I replied sobbing.

"We will try our best to guide you, dear. All we ask is that you do not give up hope!" said Lady Hall.

"I have so much I need to explain and I'm so sorry I kept secrets from you —"

"Oh my, what secrets love?" said Miriam.

"Well…"

"Carol, darling we've known all along what you were up to, however we couldn't tell you we knew. It was all written a long time and was destined." answered Miriam.

"Oh?" I sat down in the ball of light rubbing my forehead. The octopus things seemed to be ignoring our conversation and were fighting amongst themselves. I think they were furious because they couldn't get near the circle of light so they turned on each other. I was happy to ignore them and pretend they were not there. Besides what my mother was saying had me raptured. Had my full attention. First Jimmy and now them? How many other people knew this was going to happen, my dad also?"

I was jerked from my thoughts as my Godmother continued.

"Yes. It's no secret that you were meant to go on this mission darling. We fully expect you to return with Grandma Lily. I know you heard her voice and we did too and you heard me try to speak with her. We do not know from where exactly she called out."

"I felt hands touch me," I interjected.

Lady Hall added "Yes Caroline but we do not know that those hands were actually hers. What? All right, Miriam, I'll tell her. She's still got time, Miriam. Stop fretting. It will not help the child.—Carol, your mother says that she has just got some communication! You are to proceed down the tunnel and turn right. When you turn right you will approach the yellow sign that says exit, do not go through that door. Turn right, and you will approach an opening in the cave. It will say enter. Then, go in. Be prepared for anything but you must remain in the light at all times and have faith!"

I've been chased by flying bullets, octopuses about to eat me alive, and creepy, slimy bodies asking me for help, Godmother! Faith is all I have, —"

"Carol I'm losing you. Carol dear, can you hear me?" I could barely hear her now.

"No not really! Your voice is getting fainter godmother; please don't leave me and Grandma Lily alone here! Godmother! Mom, are you there?" I yelled.

I experienced complete silence after this.

"Yes darling, I love you!" cried Miriam.

"Oh, Miriam, I believe we've lost her. Carol…Carol?"

It's hard to describe the complete and utter desolation and aloneness I felt. You'd have to be there to believe it, but I'm hoping you still trust me. Remember, I'm with you all the way. Not only could I still hear those horrible sounds and groaning, but I felt like I was caged in, like some kind of wild animal. Man. So anyway, what was that all about, anyhow? Lady Hall saying, that she and my mother knew what I was up to all along. How absurd! That just blew my mind, and made feel like a complete idiot. First it was Jimmy and now them. It was like it was a conspiracy theory all along. I was the one in the dark, (except for my stage light literally which was protecting me) thinking I had been the one privy to the information—and that I had everyone else in the dark and eating out of the palm of my hand. Idiot! Thought I had everyone going along with my program. That just goes to show you. Talk about misconception and disillusionment. It wasn't until everything had come crashing down that anyone had decided to let me in on any of this. All along, it appeared that no one had been questioning my motives for the dance craze. Now I understand!

What an idiot! I felt as small as a mouse, and completely humiliated. What about my dad? Did he know too? And all those years of him reading to me the bedtime story? I certainly was deluded with thoughts of my role and importance in rescuing Grandma Lily. Or was I?

Also, ever since hearing her voice what seemed like ages ago, there'd been nothing. Not a sound, but for the awful sounds of the octopus things still fighting amongst themselves that I couldn't seem to get rid of, no matter how hard I pressed my fingers against my ears. At least they weren't touching me at the moment. The faint light I had earlier has vanished completely. How was I supposed to remain in it and follow the directions? Was I being unrealistic in thinking I could ever find—I mean, rescue Grandma Lily? What on Earth could this be all about? Maybe I was being led on in vain. I could feel my teeth clenching in upcoming anger to find myself in this predicament. How did I get out of here in this complete darkness? I was trying my hardest to keep my faith. I let out a loud scream. "I won't give up!"

Instead of perhaps my voice echoing back to me, this is what I heard.

"Put your hand in mine. I will be your light."

Talk about jumping out of my skin! "Man-bird, Rufus is that you?" I shrieked in relief, spinning around in the dark with my arms outstretched and trying to see or feel. But I still saw nothing, and I didn't feel any wings, either. However, I don't believe I've ever been happier to hear a voice!

His voice echoed back. "Man-bird? What utter silliness, child!" boomed the painfully familiar voice.

"I know... you're right, slipped out, sorry" I answered agreeably. Anything to get some help from him. "Can you please fly me out of here? I woke up from The Land of Possibilities and ended up here! Remember my Grandma Lily, you said I had a noble cause to find her, Well I heard her voice. I am God knows where, and people speak to me and I can't even see them. I feel so alone and lost. Everyone's deserted me and... where am I?"

"You are now in the Valley of the Destitute."

"The Valley of the Destitute? Well, that makes sense. They are hurting here. Man-bird I can't see you either, just like the others. If I can't see you, how do I know you're even here, to at last fly me out of this place like you did before? At least I could see you then!" I ranted on, bursting into a sobbing fit.

"...and everyone knows my secret, my mom, my Godmother and maybe even my dad... it was never a secret, I know you don't know the whole story but I feel like everyone was in on it and I'm humiliated."

"So, it's your pride that's hurt, then? That your secret's been known all along by others? Oh Carol my child, your pride will be your downfall if you let it, and it will not help you save your grandma."

"Save her? How can I save her if I can't find her? I'm presuming you came to get me, and if you know where Grandma Lily is, you'll get her as well, right? You are a powerful being! You are my hope. Unlike my godmother and my mother I know you exist on this side."

Ignoring my emotional outburst, he said, "Oh so you can't see your mother and godmother on this side, so you don't believe that they can help you?"

"Yes," I replied.

"But you trust that I can?" he said.

"Do I have a choice? You are my only hope. Unlike Lady Hall and my mom, I know you exist on this side."

"I see. So you only trust me because you're in this predicament and think you have no choice. Well, I have news for you, young lady. You do have a choice. You can choose not to trust me. It's called free will. I will be back when you 'choose' to trust me!"

"What? Are you leaving me here?" I yelled out in desperation. Things were looking up for a moment. Next thing I heard was a huge flap of feathers and wind that threw me to the ground. He really was here, not just his voice. I blew it once again with man-bird. I was so taken up with my plight. However, as he left, my protective stage light appeared once more! I was so grateful. Although he was upset he was still merciful. He must have done something to bring it back or someone did!

THE LAND OF POSSIBILITIES: JIMMY

SIXTEEN

As Jimmy awoke, he wondered what it was that woke him. It seemed he'd only rested for a short while, but it was enough. What a beautiful, amazing banquet they'd enjoyed earlier. The seraphim, (flying girls, as Carol called them—that brought a smile to his face), were presently singing their latest opera. Carol was undergoing the greatest test, and he knew all was not so well with her. At least not to her knowledge.

He'd hoped to relieve her by now of her burdens and the cross she'd had to carry, but it wasn't time yet. The Great Light would soon be sent, even though she didn't know it. Then he'd make his presence known, and she'd be blown away by what she'd see him perform. He wished things could be different, but there was nothing that could be changed. It was her destiny. She loved so very much in her imperfect way. Her love could encompass the entire Universe.

Deciding to take a walk along the banks, Jimmy strode along, always at home next to the land's amazing creation of animals. The deer, the squirrels, the bunny rabbits, the moose, the cows, the chickens, the rabbits, the dogs, the sheep, the goats, the lizards, the lions, the tigers—they were all enjoying their day, their lives. The children, the elders, the cherubim and the seraphim. How peaceful they all were. How fortunate for Carol to have been able to visit. Hopefully she'd realize it one day. What a privilege. It would be a tough decision her grandmother would be making soon. One he'd wished no one would have had to make.

Jimmy sat down next to one of the lionesses and gave her a smooch on the cheek in greeting. "What do you think?" he asked her. "Would you ever want to live anywhere else but here?"

"Rooooarr," she answered.

"Got it," laughed Jimmy. "Not in a million years."

The lioness nodded and gave him a great big lick of love.

"Well. I must be on my way Linda," said Jimmy as he sauntered off. "I must visit the Lady," he thought. "It's been too long." As he made his way to the Palace mansion, Jimmy glanced up above and thought, "How endless the sky is here, where Earth and sky meet and become one. Where all is one," he mused. He would visit the Lady, he decided. It'd been a while since he'd actually looked upon her face. He'd missed it so. Turning around the bend, Jimmy waved in greeting to the others as he passed by. He loved the way their joy was reflected in each other. It took his mind off Carol for a moment. How could he bear to say goodbye to her tomorrow?

Well, I need not worry myself about it now. All I need to do is enjoy today. Tomorrow is enough trouble in itself. With that in mind, Jimmy sauntered off once again towards the most magnificent mansion (that resembled a castle) of them all: the one where the banquet had taken place, with Carol and the cherubim only yesterday. Jimmy knew her majesty would show herself to him today.

The entrance door was so beautiful. Brocade made of pure gold and topped with every precious gem that ever existed. Just the door would make any earthly palace writhe in embarrassment.

As he entered, as always, he was greeted by the beautiful aroma of a rose bush. Her majesty was seated in her splendor upon the throne. Looking upon her face was like gazing upon a million moonbeams. So radiant…so pure! It shimmered against her skin and perfect features. Though all features were perfect in The Land of Possibilities, hers was indescribable. Her robe was royal blue silk with satin slippers to match. How he'd missed her glorious sight the past seventeen and a half years. Waltzing in excitedly, it was always this way, as if he'd never left.

Sensing his presence immediately as he entered, though her back was turned toward him, she swung that mighty chair around. "Jimmy!" She cried out "Oh how I've longed for your presence." she said beamingly. They hugged for what some would consider an eternity, in places where time existed or mattered. Disentangling herself for a moment from the hug, she curtsied.

"My lady," said Jimmy, bowing elegantly in return.

"My darling son, how I've longed to hug you again."

"Soul of my soul, spirit of my spirit," whispered Jimmy, lost in the depth of her eyes, her perfect features broke into a heavenly smile.

"We must celebrate our Carol and how far she's come!" said the Lady, popping open a bottle of chilled champagne and pouring it into two waiting flutes.

"My Lady, as we speak she is undergoing the most serious test, as you know," said Jimmy.

"Oh, but how brilliant will be the outcome," said the Lady "The destiny of so many others rides on her success—"

"And her love," interrupted Jimmy, looking down on the plush red carpet. "Though in many ways a typical teen ..."

"Her love could encompass the entire universe," finished Lady Grace.

Her statement was followed by a poignant silence that none wished to break; only the seraphim could be heard, including Humility, Generosity, Meekness, Temperance, Diligence and Chastity who were now back at their usual station - until Lady Grace announced, "Let's toast to Carol!"

"To—" said Jimmy

"Not so quick!" said an incoming voice.

"Rufus!" said Jimmy. He turned to Rufus with glee, watching him walk over and kiss Lady Grace's hand, feathery wings no longer in sight. "We didn't hear you come in," said Jimmy enthusiastically.

"As it should be, at times," he said, grabbing Jimmy to his side in a tight hug.

"Surely," Jimmy replied.

"I think I'll have some of that," said Rufus, helping himself to a dollop of bubbly from a third flute that mysteriously appeared, as things tend to do in the land. "We will drink to Carol, now that I'm here."

"So pleased to have you join us, Rufus," said Lady Grace. "We know you had to leave her for the final lessons and victory."

"To Carol!" he said, lifting his glass.

"To Carol!" said the Lady.

"To Carol!" said Jimmy.

"Now, it's time to dispatch The Great Light," announced Lady Grace.

THE VALLEY OF THE DESTITUTE

SEVENTEEN

"**E**verything is going to be fine, Grandma Lily. I promised that I'd rescue you, and that's what I'm going to do," I thought as I decided to make my way to the tunnel. I was so thankful for the protective light. I'd managed to escape the octopuses because they just couldn't get near me and I followed my mother and Lady Hall's instructions. However the protective light vanished right when I got to the exit sign. Stretching out my arms in front of me, and walked in and turned right. I took a deep breath. It was eerily quiet, almost as if the walls were testing me. "I'm going to speak to the dark, why not?" I decided without a moment's hesitation.

"Grandma Lily, I promised to rescue you and that's what I'm about to do." I shouted. "Wherever you are, I'm waiting for you to come out. Rufus said I didn't trust enough but he's wrong! I'll show him how wrong he is about me. I've come this far. If you're hearing me, Grandma Lily, listen well! I'm getting you out of this place. What had Rufus said? He'd said place my hand in the dark. Well, if he's around and keeping his word, someone will be holding my hand right now—because they're really outstretched and this place is as dark as it gets. I've heard your voice, so I know I'm close. Nothing will stop me from finding you. Jimmy's gone, and it's just me now. It sure is dark here!"

Making my way down, I stubbed my toe on something really hot and hard that clattered at my feet. "Ouch!" Stooping to feel it, I felt my hand burn at its touch. Dropping it immediately, I ventured to rub my hands against my jeans to stop the burning sensation, wishing for water.

Immediately there came a resounding bang and a flash of fire and light in front of me. The most amazing and beautiful creature was standing right there. I had to call it a creature, because I'd never seen anything like him. He was at least eight feet tall. Muscular build, wearing garments made of red and gold velvet, and boots that made me think of Greg. I'd give anything to see Greg in one of his outlandish outfits right now and feel normal again. It seemed like centuries ago that we'd all been together. I wished to hug Karen and Brittany.

Jerking back to the present, I fixed my eyes once again on the creature. He possessed a beautiful face—which looked a lot like Jimmy's, strangely enough. Covering my face to protect it from the blinding light, I couldn't even look up at him, though I felt no heat from his fire. It was more a cooling phenomenon, and startlingly, my hand no longer burned.

"Did someone ask for me?" he said in a beautiful, strong voice, looking down at me with deep, piercing black eyes.

"Ask for you?" I mimicked, ill at ease but ecstatic that I was no longer alone.

"Yes, ASK for me," he replied.

"Well..."

"Did you come across a golden plate?" he asked

"A golden plate?"

"Yes, golden plate."

"Was it hot?"

"Here, it would be," he said.

"I did stub my toe against something hard and hot that clattered and I wanted to see what it was. It may have been a plate. I mean, I couldn't really tell from the dark, plus since it was hot, I dropped it. We could look—I don't think I took many steps since. We could trace back my steps," I said, beginning to turn around

"Say no more, young lady follow me."

"But—"

"Hush, there is no need for the plate anymore and it is of no use to me. It was meant for you to find. Because of your faith in making it this far, I was dispatched. That was the first step to getting me here."

"Thanks. Who are you?" I asked.

I tried to keep up with his long strides. At least his fiery blazing light helped.

"I am The Great Light." He answered.

"Did Rufus send you?" I thought he was so disappointed in me but I see now that he continues to care. First he sent me, I believe, that protective circle of light and now you."

"Why would you say he's disappointed in you?" he asked, pausing in his strides for a few beats, which brought me a little closer.

"Well, he said that I didn't trust blindly."

"Oh?" he replied with a smile. Then, after a brief pause and a heavy sigh, he added, "And do you, Carol? Do you trust blindly when you know you should?"

"Yes."

"Before he'd said that to you, or after?"

"Always... even when I was a scared little girl, I trusted!" I said adamantly.

"I see," he said softly.

All of a sudden, the groaning sounds were back as we continued our walk. Help us, help us. My spine tingled at once, but unlike previously, nothing touched me. No cold fingers this time. Also, it sounded like they'd said a name, but was unclear.

"Are they calling out to you?" I asked The Great Light. "Can you help them? As well as help me?"

"They won't be here forever and many are being let go as we speak, even by the prayers your mother and Godmother are praying right now."

"Why are they all here suffering in pain? Have they done something wrong?

"Yes, they have and some of the things were quite awful. But let's not concern ourselves with what they've done at this point. They're already suffering because of it. Let's concern ourselves with the matters at hand," he said.

"So you must know how I ended up here? Since you were sent to help me?" I asked hopefully.

"I know why you ended up here from entering a Club Monet in downtown Manhattan New York, in an effort to locate your grandmother," he answered.

I remained quiet, though wondering how he knew that and hoping for him to continue. With no words forthcoming, I ventured to break the silence.

"I heard her voice earlier," I said to the bright light.

"Yes, you did," he replied.

"She must be here then, right?"

"Why do you think so? You heard Godmother Liz's voice as well, and she told you that she wasn't here," he said. I had to admit that he was correct.

"This tunnel is simply a passageway. Communication is possible in here from all sides, by those like your Godmother Lady Hall with specific gifts on your side of the Universe."

"Universe?" I asked.

"Uh-huh."

"How did Grandma Lily end up here?"

"The past cannot be changed. Where she's going is far more relevant. Folks on your side spend way too much time judging, the bad ones are the most precious, because they need help the most. Could you give your life for something or someone not worth a dime? You pretty much discard the message. So many are very misled," he said.

After that speech, I had nothing to compete.

"So where are we going?" I asked instead. I had no thoughts to share presently on how I could make up for the inadequacies of my fellow earthlings, except for not being judgmental myself, like I'd been many times; Ms. Rake came to mind.

"I'm taking you to the gate, and there I must leave you. From there you will be fine and everything will be made clear."

"That would be nice. I'm sure tired of being left in the dark. Literally."

We went down the tunnel a ways, walking for about thirty minutes in silence. I'd never seen anyone move with such firm purpose. He was definitely on a mission and wouldn't be messed around with. The mission was what? I hoped it was to finally take me to my grandmother but I wasn't feeling that. There had been no mention of anything like that from him so far. There wasn't much of anything said, actually, that was useful to me. No one I'd met since I left New York spoke more than a couple words at a time and were all taking me from this point to that point. They were all like connecting flights (from Rufus, then the unicorns and now The Great Light). I was beginning to think that maybe I'd spoken way more than I needed to in my lifetime, if they were anything to go by.

My feet were beginning to ache. It wasn't like I'd planned on doing all this walking through tunnels and mountains and cliffs when I'd entered that club on 42nd Street. Lady Hall had said she and my mom would try to reach me again and though I didn't know how, I hoped they would somehow.

The Great Light could light up an entire city. It was almost blinding. However, I still wouldn't wish for the previous dark over it. He was in control, and I felt completely safe with him around.

It was beginning to burn up again here, and since I was really feeling claustrophobic, I didn't know if I could take any more. At least I still wasn't hungry. This tunnel went on forever. There was just no way I could have walked for that length of time in pitch dark, with all those groaning sounds, and retained my sanity. At one point he spoke to the groaning voices and got them silent, too. He'd said, "You must be patient, my dear friends. You're not forgotten! You are loved." he said forcefully.

The moment he'd said those words the groaning stopped and I heard sighs of relief...like when rain puts out a fire.

Thank God, because not only was I happy for them but I was really becoming nauseous from the groaning and didn't want to throw up all over them as well. Their plight was bad enough without me adding that to it.

I wondered if The Great Light had ever used that fancy sword at his side. I decided to ask. Every time I asked a question, that seemed to slow him down a bit and gave me a chance to catch up, so it was win-win for me—especially since my questions were valid, intelligent ones. "Why do you have a sword? Do you ever use it?"

There was complete silence, and I was beginning to think I would be ignored while I continued my walk-run behind daddy long-legs. The silence lasted for what seemed like an eternity, other than my heavy panting and breathing. Then I breathed a sigh of relief as he stopped, and sound came out of his lit-up mouth. I mean, when he opened his mouth, it was sheer brilliance. It's like light streamed out of every single letter. There's just no way to describe it.

"I've only used it once so far, a long time ago," he said.

"Did you kill someone with it?"

"Nope, not yet." He replied.

I decided to not ask any more questions to The Great Light. But I did make a comment.

"That's good. Now I can breathe easily," I said to him.

"Kidding," I added, noting the eyebrow raise.

"Yes you can," he answered smilingly. "However some would disagree with that being good but it wasn't their choice or decision to make," he continued.

"Why do you say that?"

"Some have questioned why I didn't use it to kill a certain individual, and why he even exists, and how your universe would be much better off without him around messing things up. Because many people on Earth's lives are so messed up because of him and many would prefer if he didn't exist."

"So you could have used it on him, but didn't and he's still alive?"

"Very much so, Carol, very much so. Unfortunately for many who have not taken the time to do their part," he continued. "The sword never touched him. It was put into the ground next to him, signifying his no return. He's not allowed in The Land of Possibilities and he is very angry.

Every now and then he tries to sneak in much to his demise. So you see, Carol, this sword is part of my armor. I must wear it at all times, and be ready to use it one last time."

"And banish this terror for good!" I exclaimed.

"You're very astute, compared to plenty of seventeen-year-olds these days. Again very bright, you're blinding me."

That made me laugh, his humor had definitely shone through with that line.

"Glad the shoe's on the other foot this time."

"Who and what does he/she look like?"

"He takes many forms and disguises, but is easily recognized if one is takes the time to recognize him. Your Grandma Lily is one of those who did not take the time—or took very little, if any—and fell for one of his tricks and that's how she ended up here."

"Grandma Lily? Whoa. How did she get mixed up with him?"

"She wasn't trained to recognize him."

"Who was supposed to give her the training?" I asked angrily. I was really upset that someone hadn't done their job and robbed my dad and me of those precious years of mother and grandmother bliss.

"What if I was to say everyone...including you?"

"Me?" I said, completely taken aback and wounded. "You are full of light, but clinically insane! I wasn't even born when she was around. How could I be part of the blame?

"Simmer down and get off your high horse. That was just a test. I simply said 'what if I was to say everyone, including you."

I couldn't deny it. He was right. "Okay, that's true. I jumped the gun. But I thought you were insinuating—"

"Uh-huh...defensiveness. No one ever wants to share blame of those entrusted to them when they go astray, but all want to take the praise when they do good. You're right. You were not around and could have done nothing. However, your reaction is typical of ones wanting to point fingers and blame everyone else for what everyone needs to do for each other."

Before I could say anything else, he suddenly came to an abrupt stop, and I could see up above a yellow exit sign. I was thinking the one Godmother Lady Hall had spoken of. Also, we seemed to have come to the end of the tunnel. So lost was I in the conversation that I'd barely even noticed.

"Do you remember what she said?"

"My godmother, so you heard her?"

"I hear everything," he said simply without pretense. "Do you remember what she said to you?"

"She said do not go through the exit sign, but turn right and go through an enter sign."

"Bingo! After all you've encountered in the past eighty hours, you still have your wits about you," he said, smiling at me. I believe that was his first smile. I could have sworn I'd seen an angel! Was he an angel? I'd never seen a smile like that. He must be an angel. What could give so much light?

"You're an angel?"

"You say so, or you ask so?"

"No one gives straight answers around here," I retorted.

"Is that so?" he replied. Then after a brief moment, he appeared to be lost in thought. "This is where I must leave you, Carol," he said.

"Why doesn't that surprise me? Everyone's been leaving me since I left New York. Even my closest friend, Jimmy," I said sadly. "What am I supposed to do now?"

"You're never alone, Carol. No one ever is. I cannot accompany you any further."

"I guess if you must, you must. Bye."

"Are you forgetting something?"

"Sorry. Thank you."

"Don't worry. Everything will be okay in the end."

"Do you know how to get back to The Land of Possibilities?" I asked curiously as an idea struck me.

"Of course," he replied

"So can you take me there?" I asked enthusiastically

"I would if I could, except now is not the time."

Okay, so I had to use my back-up idea.

"I wish I knew the address of the mansion where Jimmy, the flying girls and I last were."

"What for?" he asked quizzically.

"I'd write a letter to Jimmy. We were in the biggest and most beautiful castle there like in the middle of the city. It was made of precious gems and light bounced off its walls."

"I know the one, that's where the Royal Family lives."

"So you could drop it on the doorstep or something couldn't you? I asked ferociously.

"Guess I could do that"

I would need paper and a pen or pencil?"

"Paper, pen or pencil I cannot provide to you, however, my brain works fine. Dictate your letter to me, and it will be received."

At that, bright pink light emanated from his forehead and opened up to a beautiful piece of parchment paper, like those used in former centuries. That almost threw me for a loop!

"Go ahead," he said

"For sure, geez thanks!"

As I began dictating the letter, I could see my words begin to appear on the pink light at great speed. . I could barely keep up with it. Sometimes it would appear before I'd even finished a sentence. When I was done The Great Light asked if I wanted to look it over and I said yes. I read the entire letter back in less than thirty seconds. I could get used to this! The bright light bent over and kissed me on the forehead like a butterfly. This brought my Grandma and Grandpa's fairytale story to mind somehow, and was amazingly comforting. I'd forgotten it for a while. Then The Great Light vanished with a streak of lightning.

THE LETTER

EIGHTEEN

Jimmy couldn't sleep. The letter he'd just read from Carol delivered by The Great Light was disturbing him greatly. He'd read it again.

"My dear Jimmy,
 Since you and the flying girls have disappeared, I have been through the worst time. I wish you were here. I know that I was very harsh with you and I am sorry, please forgive me. You have been the dearest friend that I could ever wish for. Sometimes I remember when we were children together and you teased me relentlessly and then the thought is immediately replaced by how we became firm friends. You, Brittany, Karen and I. Now also, our dear Greg. I hope we return to New York soon so we can continue to dance. When you and I dance the ballet it is like the music stops and we are one. I understand that you had no recollection of The Land of Possibilities while you were on Earth and as weird as it is, I accept it. I have had to accept so much in the last few days anyway, that I know now that all is indeed a possibility and nothing at times is as it seems. I thank you from the bottom of my heart! I am wonderfully blessed to have known you and you're the best. I cannot tell you the things I feel in my heart for you as my dear friend. You are like the older brother I never had! Thank you for taking me to The Land of Possibilities. I wish I could get back there for at least one second to see it one more time and say goodbye. I don't know if I need to go through there again to return to New York but I'm sure I will find out soon enough. I don't know what happened.

When I woke up in that awful place I felt abandoned by you and everyone. Also that you kept so much hidden from me. Did you also know that my mother and godmother knew all along that I moved here to New York to find Grandma Lily? Everything is so weird. I also hope you are okay and nothing terrible has happened to you. I heard my Grandma's voice at one point and then that was it. I know you said we were only gone six days but without you and your ancient hourglass (smile) here, I have no idea how long it's been. I guess no need to worry about Jeremy's once a week phone call anymore. Sure my mother will take care of that. The Great Light came to help me but he couldn't take me any further than through the tunnel in which I'd found myself. He also has many powers and said he will deliver this letter to you. It seems you all know each other and are the privileged ones to The Land of Possibilities. I hope I get to see you again and I hope that you're alright. Make what you can of this poor little letter. Perhaps in The Land of Possibilities it's translated to all I would really like to say, which is so much more than mere words can convey,

I send you all the peace and light of the entire universe and beyond,

This should be easy for The Great Light to deliver!

I remain your dear dancer and friend beyond life and eternity,

Carol

NINETEEN

I t seemed like the moment he'd vanished, I began thinking back to the last few seconds with him. I had started to speak aloud my letter to Jimmy and before I'd even started, everything was written on the parchment. Incredible!

Not having The Great Light's presence anymore threw me for another loop. I must have spent one hour with him at the most, but when he left I was completely drained, as if life force had been taken away from me. What was that all about? I fell to the ground of the tunnel and felt like I couldn't move. It was like I'd become paralyzed. I cried out in anguish, trying to move my arms and legs, but they were completely limp. I was terrified. I couldn't believe what was happening. How was I supposed to proceed if I couldn't move? I guess I could crawl. All I had to do was turn right.

I started to crawl, crying and praying very hard to Jesus. I knew Jesus had answered many of my prayers before. Not all the time but a lot of times. I hope this was one of the 'a lot of the times.' "Jesus, please don't let me be paralyzed." I prayed. At least I still had the strength to pray. Something told me I should ask him perhaps to send Rufus back or one of the unicorns. "Please send Rufus or a unicorn, or anyone." I pleaded. I couldn't believe these were the kind of things I was asking for. Things I didn't think were real or even existed a couple days ago.

"Help me, help me..." I cried. I was hoping I wasn't going to get the same response as the others; that it wasn't my time yet.

Suddenly, I saw Rufus's beautiful face smiling in front of me! It appeared for a split second and then vanished. Immediately, I once again could feel life in my bones. I was so happy, I started laughing and crying at the same time, like in the movies. Now I knew that was a real emotion and not just acting. Thank you Jesus!

Boy, did I appreciate my legs now. It was like nothing had ever happened to me these past few days. I was so filled with joy and energy. I couldn't believe the cowardly thoughts I'd had seconds after the bright being had vanished the first time, of disobeying and going through that exit sign. The temptation had definitely been there to get this nightmare done with. Maybe that's the reason I'd been unable to move.

Well, no more doubt and hesitation to fulfill my mission. I eagerly turned right in anticipation of the opening, and the enter sign that Lady Hall had mentioned and the bright being had confirmed. There it was. Let the games begin!

The moment I went through the entrance of the cave, I was immediately transported on another ride of a lifetime. I was taken up into the air and spun around like a flying trapeze or whirlpool. It was terrific! After being huddled in the tunnel with barely enough room to sneeze on either side, being in such open space was definitely appreciated.

However, it didn't last long. Suddenly I felt myself descend and approach a deep hole about five feet wide, and the sheer force was sucking me in. I descended into the ground as it opened up to welcome me. That was terrifying but I wasn't paralyzed and that was good enough.

Seconds later, I landed in the midst of a community. I was thinking Grandma Lily's perhaps? It was about time. First thing I noticed was that this place was as dark as the tunnel. Oh, no! Rephrase. More terrifying. Wait. I thought I saw—oh, yes. Alas, my stage light was back. There was a sole light that surrounded me once again and helped me to see. Maybe I'd garnered a halo through positive energy? I was definitely of the belief anything was possible at this point.

The inhabitants seemed extremely busy and loud, from what I could see, even more than New York City and completely opposite to the Land of Possibilities, where everyone there was relaxed and looked like nothing mattered. No one appeared to notice me at first, which was weird, since having come to the realization that I hadn't been paralyzed, I was so bouncy and knew I was oozing out tons of positive energy and vibrations. Which I must tell you was completely opposite to what I was hearing and feeling there. Perhaps I was invisible again? I also noticed I was surrounded by my circle of light once again! Maybe I was invisible to them like I was in the Land Of Possibilities.

I observed them quietly some more.

These were some angry folks, ugly folks. They were either yelling obscenities at the tops of their lungs, or in bloody brawl fights. They were also sweating buckets. Maybe that had something to do with the bonfires—or fire pits, I should say, that were everywhere. I have good memories of bonfires, especially at the beach. Don't want to change that image.

I hid behind what looked like the sole tree in the middle of the courtyard I'd found myself in. This place was barren, I tell you, barren. That tree was completely out of place. I gave it a hug, since it wasn't fighting or cursing. Was it also keeping me cool? I was the only one not sweating. So far I hadn't noticed any children. Good thing. This place was not for kids—or more so, for anyone. That was very weird. To have all those people there, yet no children?

There was a light beam for a second (as I was getting used to having now and then) but no bright being appeared this time, and I saw what I'd mistaken for busyness was actually bloody fights. This place was far worse than the Land of the Destitute. Suddenly I heard Rufus's voice "You've been given a glimpse, Carol of The Isle of The Hopeless and were descended there briefly."

"Rufus you're here?" I yelled excitedly.

"Yes, sort of –"

Cutting him off

"Please are you here to fly me out of here and take me to my grandma finally?"

"Not quite yet but you will be out of here soon."

"Geez thanks for the good news," I replied bummed out. "When then?"

"As soon as you remember you are not one of them. Not without hope."

"I see."

Hope came quickly.

The other light beam darted for a second and was gone.

"Bye Rufus," I said out loud, sadly.

I looked around. The community seemed to go on and on. I wondered how many people lived there, and if they were all acting out in the same way. As I hid behind the tree, I could overhear the conversation of the group who were in the brawl fight nearest to me. It seemed they hated everyone and everything. I couldn't get out of there fast enough!

I filled up my spirit with hope, and my positive vibrations must have put me back in full throttle—for immediately when I wished that I could be gone, the tree and I were uplifted and taken off the ground. I mean, it was uprooted while I was embraced in my tree hug, and next thing I knew we were both heading off to somewhere. God alone knew where now. I wished for The Land of Possibilities, but Grandma Lily still needed to be rescued.

Well, I'd go anywhere with that tree to be gone from where I was. I had no clue what kind of tree it was. Seemed out of place there, but I was holding on to it for dear life. At this point I'd gone from hugging it to swinging on one of its branches like a monkey.

No sooner had we gone up into the air, my circle of light was gone and I was in pitch dark. Again, I hit my head against something hard and saw stars. Just like in a cartoon. That stuff was real, after all. That was the last thing I remembered until I woke up next to a tiny little pond.

For the first time in my life, I missed no one. I had my tree, the pond and myself. I'd begun to refer to it as my tree now, since we seemed to be stuck to one another like white on rice. I'll just lay there at this little pond forever.

I was still oozing out my positive vibrations. The lump on my head was a reminder of what had happened previously, and where I'd been and what I'd witnessed, but nothing could get me down now. I felt really sorry for the inhabitants of that previous place 'The Isle of The Hopeless', but there was nothing I could do about it to help them. I would focus on the things and people that I could help.

I was really going to be a better person when I returned to my old life, I thought. I knew that my view of life had drastically changed. I was especially going to be a better big sister to Jeremy. I wanted to finally let go of my obsession of finding Grandma Lily, because every time I thought I was closer, I was nothing but further away. I thought I'd just stay positive and let nature take its course.

I made a conscious effort to let all thoughts of finding her go. Then I closed my eyes and drifted to sleep.

When I woke up, there were three pairs of eyes hovering over me. Whoa! But they were kind eyes, so I wasn't scared. They were obviously waiting for me to wake up. They were two girls and a boy. Perhaps teenagers like me, though their eyes looked old beyond their years. There were two girls and one boy. The only difference was our clothes. They wore animal fur and skin. I could actually smell it. They also spoke a different language, which I could not comprehend. They were looking at me quizzically, like I was an alien or something. I'm sure to them, I was. I gestured that I could not understand a word.

"English," I said.

Immediately one of the girls nodded in excited acknowledgment of my request. I guess this was her big chance to practice?

"Oh, yes," she said. She was pretty excited. Something told me she didn't get to use it much.

"We're wondering how you got here," she said.

"A bump on the head and a tree," I replied, pointing at my tree. That drew in some laughter, especially after she'd translated to the other two.

"Who are you, and where am I?" I asked her.

"We are not allowed to tell strangers of our nationality, or anything else about us, but we can show you around and introduce you to the others. You are in The Land of the Destitute. Come with us."

Okay, back in the Land of the Destitute. But this was a nice spot. There was no groaning here.

"Well... I'm really beginning to enjoy my time here at this little pond with my tree, and I must let you know that I have had plenty of adventure the past few days, and could use a time out," I said.

"You are not going to be able to just stay here at this pond indefinitely. Visitors are usually here for a purpose, with little time to spare. I believe you are being lulled into a false sense of security. So if I were you, I'd keep moving. Something has brought you here, and I doubt it's to lay here at the river bank," she said, translating all the while to the others. She was really talented. They all nodded and said some words to her. She did not translate it.

"What did they say?" I asked.

"They say that you are here because someone's time is up, and that person will be leaving with you. That's usually when we get visitors."

"Someone's time is up?" I remembered The Great Light's words to some of the groaners. 'Your time isn't up yet.' So Grandma Lily's time must be up.

"You are here to pick up someone, yes?"

"Oh yes, I am!" I exclaimed, with all my energy, excitement and Grandma Lily obsession returning full throttle." Do you know someone by the name of Lily?" I asked exuberantly.

She told the others. All three drew a blank, looking at each other for clarification. "No one we know of," said the one who spoke English. "Are you sure she's the one you're here to pick up?"

Really disappointed, I held my head in both my hands and felt really tired. This positive thing was tough in face of another disappointment.

"Yes," I said

"Well then, just because we haven't heard of her, doesn't mean she isn't here. We don't know everyone," she said. "Cheer up!"

That perked me up. Well, why didn't you just say so? I thought, immediately bouncing up at once with a spring in my step. I proceeded to go with them. I thought that was a good idea.

They seemed to know more than I did, and they were right. I wasn't getting any closer to my goal lying here by the pond as comforting as it was.

"There are many different parts of The Land of The Destitute and many different communities and lifestyles."

"Oh, I see…like this peaceful spot here at the pond?"

"Yes, exactly." she replied

"Did you have to go through the town of the groaners?"

"Yes I did," I replied, as the memory brought a chill up my spine.

She must have seen me shiver.

"Really awful wasn't it?" she said sympathetically.

I nodded. "What are your names?" I asked, changing the subject intentionally.

"I'm Jasmine, and they're Sage and Rose," she replied, referring to the other two.

🝔🝔🝔

"I'm Carol, and my tree goes with me," I said to them, pointing at it.

"What do you mean?" asked Jasmine, giving me an incredulous look. "Goes with you?"

"We've been traveling together for a little while," I said, hoping they didn't think I was crazy.

Jasmine shrugging her shoulders and glancing at the others, said to me, "If you say so."

I started walking, and to my dismay, my tree didn't move anymore. I even started speaking to it. Now they really thought I was loony. I received no response. I hugged it goodbye. Jasmine, Sage and Rose chuckled.

"So, how long have you lived here?" I asked Jasmine.

"Quite a long time, hundreds of years."

I was stupefied. "Hundreds of years, what do you mean? You aren't hundreds of years old!"

"How do you know how old we are?"

"Well, you look so young and-" I trailed off. Why am I even answering? For a moment, Ms. Gilroy from elementary school came to mind. I hadn't thought of her in a while. She'd fit right in here.

"Yes we do but that is not so important now, miss."

She had a point.

We ventured out about a mile or two, after which we approached a hill. Then we climbed to the top and happened on some people involved in an animated discussion. They were speaking the language of my tour guides. They were seated around a fire, and although it was still light, the fire gave off a special kind of light.

"These are the elders," said Jasmine as we approached them. Bowing, she greeted them, followed by Sage and Rose. There must have been fifty of them or so. They were a mixture of men and women. The men were smoking cigars, and the women were making stuff out of wool, though they were all engaged in conversation.

One of the men stood up when he saw us and started walking toward me. As he approached me, I held out my hand to shake his, following Jasmine and the others' lead. He knelt down at my feet. I was astonished and extremely taken aback. I did not know what to make of it, and what my response to such an outlandish gesture should be. Jasmine gave me an incredulous look, and I gathered she was lost as well, and didn't know what to make of me. After he knelt at my feet, he took my hand and kissed it. I was completely startled and didn't know what to say. He said some words to Jasmine, and after giving her an enquiring look, she said to me, "He said that we have been waiting for your visit, your Royal Highness."

"Who do they think I am?"

"Not who they think you are. Who you are," she said.

"Who am I?"

"They believe you to be of royal blood, a princess descended from a royal line of families in The Land of Possibilities."

"Jasmine, I don't know what these folks eat or drink out here in The Valley of The Destitute that would make them think such a thing but I am Carol, a teenager studying dance in New York."

Belting out hysterical laughter, she was clearly humored.

"What? It's not funny!" I said to Jasmine. "Tell him he's mistaken. I am not of any royal blood."

Jasmine then beckoned to an aide at the side of the elder, he approached me. He spoke English. "Speak to him," she said.

I repeated what I'd just told Jasmine to him.

He turned to him and told him what I'd said.

Then he told me what Mustafa's response was. "He says utter nonsense, and yes you are a princess." Afterward, all fifty or so of them proceeded to bow to me and kiss my hand. Even more amazingly, Jasmine, Sage and Rose followed suit. I could see in their faces that they were wondering how this crazy person who spoke to trees could be royalty. They need not worry. I was thinking the same of myself, and I knew these people were mistaken.

As I was thinking these thoughts, the first man or elder Mustafa who had bowed to me started giving instructions. I knew they pertained to me, for immediately one of the women got up and took me by the hand, and brought me into a nearby tent. It looked comfortable and was nicely set up inside. Jasmine accompanied us and said the women had said that I could have a bath, and help myself to some of her clothing. Jasmine looked at me quizzically, as if she herself couldn't believe what was happening. After the woman had left the tent, I was able to ask her what she was thinking.

"I've decided to take a break from thinking," was her response.

I let it drop.

After my bath and shower, I found clothing and slippers laid out for me. After dressing myself, I went out of the tent to join the others. I couldn't believe my eyes.

There must have been a thousand people gathered.

"They've come from all over The Land of The Destitute to see you, even some groaners were able to get away-which is shocking," said Jasmine, eyeing me cautiously with Sage and Rose at her side. I'm getting she didn't buy the whole royalty thing, especially since she'd seen me speak to a tree.

"Why?" I asked her.

"Because you're royalty, of course," she said.

TWENTY

"**M**y friends, today we have in our midst a royal visitor that we've been waiting for a very long time from the other side. She came with no servants, maidens, carriages, or diamonds and rubies, but royalty she is! We do not know how long she'll be with us, but for however long, we need to make her feel welcome and appreciated, and learn all that we can from her on how to get to her side of town." They all started laughing.

"Shhhh," he continued. "As you all know, this is no laughing matter. Some of us have been here five days, five months, twenty years, two hundred years and more. No matter how long we've been here is irrelevant. We all long to leave and go where we know we belong. We have hope! That's kept us going. Without hope we'd be nothing, and our plight would be much worse. We would be desolate and still full of every evil. Having her royal highness here reminds us that our hope is not in vain, and we too will cross the bridge to our ultimate destiny and freedom!"

"Yay!" They all belted out in response.

I was still completely lost and had no idea what was going on, or why these people think I'm royalty. There was no way I was going to let this get to me—and besides, they were bound to find out the truth. Then what?

After letting them quiet down, he continued. "We must continue to believe we will enter The Land of Possibilities, our ultimate destination. She is living proof of this." They all cheered and started waving little flags in my direction. Freedom flags? I was so nervous. I thought they'd be bound to notice at some point and started yelling fraud and throwing sticks at me. Even my smile felt like it was plastered on. "The Elders and I will be in discussion with her royal highness most of the time she's with us, but we are all equal here, and you all will be given the chance to speak with her as well." I noticed Jasmine still eyed me suspiciously. Sage and Rose, I thought didn't appear at all leery of me though, which I hope could work in my favor. They appeared oblivious to her seeming distrust of me and were hanging on the elder's every word. He continued, "Now, you all know that usually when we have a visitor, the visitor has come to take one of us to The Land of Possibilities. But this is no regular visitor. She claims she's here to do just that, as tradition would have it, but we have never been able to see a visitor pick up someone before. The princess is clearly suffering from amnesia. You may have noticed the bump on her head. So I believe she was sent here for another purpose, one even bigger than she is aware. She's just a young girl, but we know the King's messengers have often been the young and little children. Well, I think I've spoken enough now. I will let you get on with your day. It's not necessary to form any lines. Just approach her royal highness when you see she's available."

They all clapped and went about their business as usual. I think they were smarter than the elders.

I learned that the leader's name was Mustafa. Afterward, he invited me into the tent with nine of the other elders. There were him, three other men, and five women. We sat on the floor on some comfortable embroidered cushions. At first they started to speak amongst themselves, and since I didn't speak the language, I didn't participate for a while. It gave me a chance to observe them some more, very carefully. I still hadn't figured out what they'd meant by saying that they'd been here all those years. For some who were older it may have been possible, maybe, but for the younger ones—well, it just didn't make any sense to me and was difficult to comprehend.

What of all the royalty talk about me? If I was royalty, wouldn't I know? A princess —I would have been raised in a palace, with servants and a nightly court. Unless I was delusional, I didn't recall any such things growing up. Well, I'd done all I could to convince them it was impossible, and I was growing tired of singing the same song over and over again. I wasn't about to become a broken record.

Looking around me, I noticed that they were a very still people, not much movement, and they moved very slowly, even the younger ones. The women were sitting on the cushions with their arms and legs folded and humming. The men were all doing the same, except when they were conversing with Mustafa. They barely spoke to one another. They moved silently and unhurriedly, but without the peace and serenity of the inhabitants of The Land of Possibilities. It's as if they were waiting and paying attention for something to occur, some great event. I preferred not to be still too long.

"I know that there are many here but have any of you heard of Lily Brandt?" I ventured to ask Mustafa's interpreter.

"Has anyone heard of Lily Brandt?" he repeated in their language. They all shook their heads, asserting the negative.

"Who is she?" he asked.

"My grandmother on my father's side," I said.

"She may have changed her name. Many like to do this when they are here. So if she's one of those who go by another name, she's the only one who could respond, because she alone would know what her former name was."

"Great," I said. It was all beginning to sink in. "So unless she hears me ask for her, there's no way any of you would have known her by that name?"

"Exactly, also when the names are changed, they're never English names. It's always in the language of the Valley of The Destitute, Ikewa."

"I guess Jasmine, Sage and Rose kept their English names."

"Who?"

"Jasmine, Sage and Rose. They are the three teenagers that brought me to you," I replied.

"Brought you to us?"

"Yes, don't you remember them?"

"I've never heard of them. You came to us on your own."

"They were with me all the time, since I've been here, two girls and a boy."

"That bump on your head sure did a number on you dear."

"What are you talking about? They're outside," I said, hurrying out to call out to Jasmine. "Jasmine!" I yelled. "Where are you? Sage, Rose!"

I ran outside the tent with all ten following behind me. Some of the inhabitants outside turned around to look for a minute and then continued what they were doing with steady, slow motions and ignored me. It was business as usual. Was that any way to treat royalty? There were no signs of Jasmine, Sage or Rose. I again tried to tell the interpreter and described what they looked like. He told the others, including Mustafa, but they all drew blank stares.

I had to sit for a minute. I was finding it hard to breathe. My three friends were gone. I couldn't believe it. No one had seen them. They'd been invisible. Just like our hosts at the banquet had made themselves invisible, and even I had been for a little while. So I guess it was definitely possible. I really liked those three, even Jasmine, who'd thrown daggers at me.

❀❀❀

They began asking me questions about The Land of Possibilities. They all were hoping to go there. The fact that I'd been there and now was spending time with them was a really big deal. Apparently Mustafa, who sees things the others don't, had also seen a diamond and pearl tiara on my head, when I'd made my entrance and that's why he claimed I'm royalty. Other than that, there was no living proof that I am aware of. He also said it was a special tiara and one that only a special segment of royalty wore.

They all asked me to describe what it was like over there, and I did the best I could to describe what I'd observed in my brief stay. There were oohs and sighs and teary eyes. The Land of Possibilities was where they were all heading, they told me.

"Why don't you all just go there?" I asked somewhat naively. I mean, I really didn't know what was stopping them, seeing I'd visited both on the same trip. I know I'd had no luck getting back there on my own either so I was not being realistic. Clearly the fact that I had been able to visit there was a stroke of fate.

"Very stiff migration laws." he said to me half joking.

"Oh?" I said.

"If only it was that simple. Making light of it maintains our sanity," he added sincerely and sadly. "Manmade regulations would be much easier to confront. There is no way we can go there on our own. Someone has to pick us up. If you'd come to get one of us, you and they would have been long gone. You'd only have spent seconds here. As it is, the one you've come to find has not yet revealed her-self to you fully, and there's nothing you can do in the meantime but wait. While you do so, we will enjoy your company and the sharing of your time in The Land of Possibilities. We can never hear or get enough stories of there, even if you were to stay here a thousand years." That had me wincing.

"All the others outside are yearning to speak with you, but it is so painful for them to hear of it, and to be here and not there, that they can hardly bear it. Do not feel offended by their behavior, whatsoever. We the elders have garnered a bit more grace, by no means of ourselves of course, so we are able to rise above our pain and listen to the stories you tell of there. The others will come soon, but they are not yet prepared. As soon as they are, there will be long lines at your feet each day, for even just one word of the land. Mark my words. You must speak to each individually, because each will need to get their understanding from your voice. What I'd said in my speech earlier, that there was no need for them to form lines that was another small joke."

The time that the others were ready came quite unexpectedly, but not too soon for me. For about an hour I shared with the elders my experiences in the Land of Possibilities, Rufus, the unicorns, the beautiful trees, the magnificent flowers, rainbows, beaches, the happiness of the inhabitants, etc. I asked to excuse myself to get some air outside the tent. As soon as I'd exited the tent, there was a line the length of I don't know, maybe a thousand miles, outside! The girl in front place, who looked around sixteen years old, looked up at me with teary eyes and said meekly, "I'd like you to tell me about the Land of Possibilities, please, your royal highness." That title still took some getting used to.

"Sure," I replied.

Then one by one, I told them each what I could recall. I had no idea where the energy came from, but I'd lost count of how many I'd spoken to, young and old. At some point, someone came out and said to them it was enough for today. The others who were still lined up obediently went away. I wondered what was going to take place tomorrow.

Though I'd lost track of time, I was really thinking time was almost up. Jimmy had said we had six days to get back to New York, and something told me it was getting very close. How was I

to get back? I did not yet know. Perhaps there would be more gunshots. I was not looking forward to that. The last time could have been sheer luck and a narrow escape.

I went back into the tent, laid down and went to sleep. When I awoke, I couldn't believe my eyes. Jasmine, Sage and Rose were back—just like they'd been when I'd awakened by the river bank!

'Hi!" I exclaimed. "You're back! You three disappeared on me and made me look like an idiot! All the locals thought I was nuts speaking of you!"

"Calm down," said Jasmine smugly. "We had to. We needed to verify some things about you. Especially the royalty notion. We were not told anything like that beforehand, which is not unusual. Now we are back to continue our angel mission—"

"Angel mission? Are you angels?" I asked excitedly.

"We are. We are guardian angels, you get three of us for this leg of your mission, although usually you have just Sage," she said matter-of-factly.

"Oh?' I turned to look at Sage, who just smiled.

"Thanks," I said to him, eyeing him quizzically. It's not every day one gets to see their guardian angel, if it was indeed true. Neat.

"What else did you think we were? Magicians?"

"Well—" I stammered. "You don't look like angels and you have no wings."

"Unimportant. I had to confirm for myself that you were what they were making you out to be and I am satisfied now. Rose had to accompany me. Sage was always at your side, as usual."

"So, how has your time in the Land of The Destitute been so far?" Jasmine asked.

"It's been interesting, to say the least. So what did you learn about me when you were gone? Am I really some kind of princess?"

"You are royalty. What station is irrelevant."

"Are you for real?" I interjected. I was finding that hard to believe but somewhat thrilling.

Jasmine must have read my mind or outburst and she put a damper on my thrill with her next statement.

"But if I were you, I wouldn't let it go to your head. So are we. You must leave now with us, though. Don't think of saying goodbye. There is none needed," she continued. I noticed a few of the female elders who I was sharing the tent with turned to look at me for a moment when they heard me murmuring, but then since I'd mentioned having three invisible friends before, they paid no attention and went about their knitting. I guessed Jasmine, Rose and Sage were once again unseen. "Pay no attention, they already believe you to be crazy royalty," she said.

"Yeah, no thanks to you," I replied. That had Rose giggling, though Sage kept a straight face. He was such a boy, I mean boy angel. I had to admit it was nice to have them back.

"So, where are you taking me?" I asked suspiciously.

"You're not exactly leaving the Land of Destitute yet, but there is just another part that you need to go through."

"Is Grandma Lily there?"

"We aren't told everything, as we already explained. We're only told what our duties are."

"So what will everyone think, when they notice I'm gone?"

"They won't think anything except that the same way you unexpectedly arrived is the same way you've left."

"There are lots of people left who were waiting in line for stories of the Land Of Possibilities, who haven't heard about it yet from me. Won't they be disappointed that I'm gone without a word?" I asked wearily.

"My, my, you already believe yourself to be indispensable in such a short time? Some of those who you are worrying about have already gone on to the Land Of Possibilities by now and no longer need stories. They are living their dream. The poor souls still left behind must wait their turn. You may be pleased to know that Mustafa has already gone on as well. Someone came just five minutes ago to get him. Guess his last gig here was you. Usually the ones who've come to get those ready to move on from here are also invisible. You were the first actually seen. That's why you were treated with such awe. Not to mention your invisible tiara. You are a special case. Let's go!" she commanded.

As soon as she'd said the words, I felt my body move in a spiral twist, and next thing I knew the four of us landed on a high mountain.

"We will not be leaving you this time," said Jasmine, seconds afterwards. "However, we will remain invisible to the others, and at times to you as well, but make no mistake—we are here. Do not be afraid!"

With these words they all three vanished into thin air. Once again, I was bemused and didn't know what to expect. Glancing around me, all I could think was, man, I was in the pits. What's up with leaving me here on my own again? Those angels were crazy. Well, they said they'd still be around, though back to invisibility, their favorite and most common state.

Suddenly I noticed a ton of those octopus beasts coming toward me and I started running down the mountain. I could barely see in front of me. I could see nothing but a speck of light, that's all, and there must've been hundreds of them! I couldn't run fast enough to lose them. As I raced down the mountain, I noticed perhaps thousands in the distance. I couldn't turn around. There were others behind. I wish Rufus could be here, like last time (It seems I was always wishing for Rufus). Those angels seemed to be asleep on the job right now.

What should I do—suddenly some of them started turning back running and I saw why. They were being shot down by arrows and some were looking to escape that fate. Fantastic! But how about the ones behind me?

Then out of nowhere appearing on the ground before me was that golden plate I had stubbed my foot on when The Great Light had appeared. I decided to kick it this time intentionally. I was desperate and I hoped it would bring the Great Light again. He appeared briefly for a moment standing in front of me! It was so quick and it was like I'd imagined it. Then he disappeared.

But then these other octopus looking beasts things started running in the other direction. Amazing...this disc works! Thank you, Great Light.

When they left, I ran to pick up the golden disc. I had no idea what this thing was, but I'd see what it does and I was holding onto it. After all that running back and forth, I had to sit down and catch my breath.

I was feeling really desolate now, and I missed my family. I missed home, and I was tired.

"Grandma Lily!" I shouted at the top of my lungs as loud as possibly could. My voice echoed back. Did not surprise me.

"Where are you? I've been through enough now! All I wanted to do was find you. I thought you were in New York, and that's been nothing but a joke. Grandma Lily!" I yelled out again, and all I could hear was my voice echoing back at me. It was useless.

EARTH

TWENTY-ONE

"**L**iz, Liz, wake up!" yelled Miriam frantically. She was in a panic state. For the first time, she was able to see her daughter in The Valley of The Destitute on her quest to return her Grandma Lily to Earth, for the sake of love for her father. The sight of her being chased had haunted her dreadfully, as was her helplessness to do something drastic to help. As a mother, that was probably the most highly frustrating, to say the least.

"What is it, dear?" shouted Lady Hall from the chaise she was lounging in.

"It's Carol. I can see her, Lady Hall. I can see her! I'm frightened beyond my wits for her. Is there anything more that we can do but pray?"

"Oh, dear Miriam, there is nothing more powerful than prayer. There may be a number of other things that we can do, but none more powerful. Not remotely! I'm overjoyed that you were able to see our dear girl at last on the other side. You were granted the privilege that I've been privy to all of my life. How wonderful! It's a miracle as well as the moment we've all been waiting. It is also a sign she needs even more of our prayers at this crucial time. The moment is now for us to pray even harder for Her Majesty to intervene and put Lily's misery to rest."

They prayed for the next two hours without stopping. When they thought they'd prayed as much as they could, they were beginning to feel really tired. Lady Hall said to Miriam,

"Why don't you take a break dear? A good soak in the tub should do it. It's also so awfully hot in here today. Times like these sure make me wish for the London cold. Oh, who am I kidding—I am home here. A cold drink would do an old woman a lot of good right now. Some good old-fashioned American iced tea should do the trick."

Miriam had no choice but to chuckle at that.

"I could use some ice tea myself, I'll make some." She replied, yawning. "This heat sure makes me sleepy."

"You're sweating profusely too, dear. I recommend a cold soak."

"Uhhh…I don't think so, weird lady, warm will do," answered Miriam laughing for the first time in days. Lady Hall laughed back.

"By the way, how's little Jeremy?" she asked to change the subject to more pressing matters at hand. You must bring him by soon. I know he misses Carol, and I hope you aren't treating him as an only child since she's been away. It's his greatest fear, you know. He truly dreads that."

"Really?" said Miriam. Highly surprised at this news of Jeremy's secret fear, and no less surprised at Lady Hall's sixth sense, she said, "How do you know? Stupid question, of course, I'll do my best."

"What interesting children you and Marc have brought into the world dear. Marc? how about him? How's he handling Carol's being gone?"

"It's hard to say. I believe he's beginning to spoil Jeremy. Yesterday he let him have three ice cream cones," said Miriam, handing Lady Hall a glass of iced tea.

"Thanks dear," she said as she took the glass from Miriam and added, "Dreadful. Jeremy was only testing him. Poor Jeremy, he's already beginning to feel like an only child—albeit if nature had made it so, he'd be left with no choice. You must speak with Marc at the earliest. However as we speak Jeremy is also praying Carol leaves New York soon and returns home…especially since the triple ice cream experience." He has her location wrong but his prayers are very strong.

THE LADY

All of a sudden it looked as if the sky was about to fall. The sun started spinning above and turned a bright purple color, and then various colors of blues. There were also oranges and a hint of yellow. It was the most incredible sight I'd ever seen. There was a thunderous noise, and I stood there dumbstruck. I had no idea what was taking place. Of all the incredulous things I'd witnessed since entering that club on 42nd Street with Jimmy, this was by far the most unbelievable sight of them all. I was completely struck with awe at what I was seeing.

After this, the sky opened up and a woman descended from it, surrounded by beautiful half-naked babies that were all floating around her. They were cherubs! I'd seen them in photos, so I knew what they were. There were many. They were singing the most beautiful classical music. Some had flutes, others harps and violins, others trumpets.

Then I saw the woman smile at me as she continued to get closer. She was amazingly pretty. She was wearing a flowing robe, like we were given at dinner in The Land of Possibilities, except hers was made of pure white silk. As she got really close, she hovered above the top of my head, facing me, suspended in thin air. She was so bright, I was thinking I'd be blinded, but somehow I was able to look at her. There were no words spoken by her, and neither I, of course.

"Shush," she said to me as she placed her forefinger on her lips. "Do not worry for the moment of who I am. I am here to help you," was her reply. "I know you've come a long way but I must let you know that you are also right on time. Your timing is perfect, for your grandmother's reached the end of her time here, Carol."

So she knew my name. "Huh?" was all I could seem to muster. It was as if someone else was talking. I was still trying to comprehend this vision of a woman in front of me. Her skin was glowing light, and her hair was like it was on fire, a burning copper red. She must have been at least ten feet tall. I felt as small as an ant. Now I know how they felt.

She was smiling sweetly. I should try smiling back. I decided to try this again. Maybe who she was, wasn't as important as what she could do, or do for me.

"Hi," I smiled at her.

After I smiled her eyes lit up like moonbeams.

"I am Lady Grace." She said.

Oh, I thought. She looked like the real deal.

Immediately afterward, I saw the ground open below her.

THE DESCENT

S hortly following was the most filthy of odors you could ever have the misfortune of smelling. I swear I would have been knocked out by the stench, but I was still too caught up in her vision of gloriousness. The filth came boiling up to the surface in the form of mud, grime, slime, molten lava. It was steaming. Any and every gross substance was protruding out. Then it suspended in the air briefly, spun like a whirlpool. I caught a glimpse of faces in the mire. None of whom I recognized, thankfully! Still, I couldn't believe what I was seeing.

Then the beautiful lady, feet down, descended into the awful whirlpool of grime. Oh, man. I just couldn't believe my eyes. The cherubs were still singing and hovering above her. Were those cuties going in, too? That would be the worst. I closed my eyes. I couldn't bear to look. When I opened them up seconds later, they were all gone, so I guess they did go into it. Go into such filth? I was completely stunned and nauseous at the same time, and felt I would pass out at any moment from the sight and the stench.

I closed my eyes again and began to back up in terror. I dared not go too close, in case I was sucked in the whirlpool also and to be seen no more. Forget being seen no more—I would stink for a lifetime. I could never get rid of a stench like that. That perfume or bath soap has not yet been invented.

Before I had time to go very far, I saw the beautiful lady and the cherubs return out of the filthy whirlpool. I wouldn't dare look, but then they were back as beautiful and as clean as ever and didn't even smell. That was insane.

Along with her and the cherubs, was a woman hanging onto her arm. Clean and wearing a squeaky white gown. She was a funny-looking thing. Also, she looked so strikingly familiar that it was uncanny. I tried to put my finger on it, but I was stumped. Then it hit me—she looked a lot like me, just an older version. This was incredible. Then she'd have to be...could it possibly be?

It had to be her! There was no other way to explain the resemblance. She looked exactly like a female version of my dad—who, as you know, I take after. I looked at her, and our eyes met. She was eyeing me very keenly, and we looked deep into each other's eyes. This was my blood.

"Grandma Lily?" I exclaimed exuberantly, though I was shaking like a leaf in winter. I was so excited and overjoyed, I could hardly contain myself. This was beyond thrilling. She still looked at me, saying nothing. It was as though time had stood still. It seemed like an eternity went by. Then she smiled at me, the same half-smile my dad gives at times: the one which had broken my heart over and over again, and was the reason I ended up here in the first place.

She winked and said, "Yes, Carol, it's me, your Grandma Lily. It's so nice to meet you finally. I am so grateful to you Lady Grace," she said turning towards the beautiful lady and giving her a bow.

Lady Grace bowed her head in return with a graceful tilt.

Turning back toward me she continued.

"And to you my dear child you are so brave. I will spend the rest of my life thanking you." I am so sorry about that false alarm, the other day when I touched you. It was all I got to do."

Was she apologizing to me? I wasn't hearing that. There was nothing she could do wrong.

At that moment she began to make her way toward me, but I couldn't wait. I was the young and agile one, right? Well, that was the reason I gave myself for my Olympic sprint toward her, though she didn't look old. When I got to her, I hugged her tightly. I never wished to let her go until I'd brought her to my father. All my life I'd waited for this moment to arrive. I'd dreamed it, and it was finally here!

I looked at the beautiful woman who had brought her to me and love welled up in the depths of my soul and tears of joy welled up in my eyes. How grateful I was to her! How could I ever repay her? That was the question. "How can I ever repay you?" I asked, turning round toward her.

She again gracefully tilted her head at me as well, in acknowledgement of my gratitude like she'd done Grandma Lily, though added. "Thank you is enough. I do not need repayment dear. Your love is enough and you will have much opportunity to show thanks to whom it is really due. Your grandmother has just been retrieved from the worst part of the Valley of The Destitute that not too many even know exists; the underground, though she was with the groaners for a short time where she tried to reach out to you."

I had so many questions that were still unanswered. Where would I begin? All of it could wait, I imagined. I just needed to embrace this moment with everything that was in my being and cherish it forever. The moment that I was finally face to face with Grandma Lily! I couldn't take my eyes off her.

I started rambling. "Is it really you, finally?" I asked breathlessly, hardly able to sustain my excitement. And why should I? This was the moment I'd been dreaming of.

"Let's take a good look at you," she said, pulling me back and examining me from head to toe. "You are beautiful, and you look like your dad, my dear boy. How I long to hold him—and you, my dear, dear, dearest and only granddaughter. Carol, you are quite a young lady," she said, smiling at me. "You've come a long way to find me. You were able to cross the bridges that divided the earthly and spiritual worlds without being any part of madness that got me here in the first place. Not an easy feat!" she said to me proudly. I was beaming.

"We must go now," said the beautiful lady gently and softly, taking me out of my reverie. "Your Grandma Lily has been here long enough and I'm sure is anxious to leave, now that she can. And you, young lady, are due back in New York in the morning!"

"Oh," I said. New York was the last thing on my mind right now and seemed so far away. The next I knew, the beautiful lady took me by her left hand. She was still holding hands with Grandma Lily on her right. Suddenly, all three of us were whisked up into the air and ascending into the sky, just like a great air balloon, except there was no balloon. I closed my eyes as we got higher and higher up into the Universe. I was not looking down. No way! But perhaps sideways?

I turned to eye Grandma Lily. I still had to pinch myself that she was here. Who'd a thought it? Grandma Lily didn't look scared at all, just deliriously happy, maybe even more than I was. Was that even possible? Nah...

"Where are we heading?" I asked the beautiful lady.

❁❁❁

"Our first stop will be The Land of Possibilities," she replied simply. "Your Grandma Lily's never been there, but you have."

"Yes, I love it there. I had the best time ever. It was absolutely surreal and I really wanted to see it again before I returned to America with Grandma. I didn't know anywhere could be so peaceful. That was the last time I saw my friend Jimmy. Maybe he's still over there."

"Maybe so," she said. "You will soon find out."

"I don't blame him for staying, if he did. I would have. I was given no choice! I guess it was my fate to find Grandma Lily."

"I have spent all my life with Jimmy. I know that the two of you are great friends. It was very important that you two grew up together. In fact, your twin friends were also very essential in rescuing Grandma Lily. They were your support group. It is important that friends build each other up, and the four of you did just that. Congratulations! Well done."

"Thank you!" I said with joy. I was deliriously happy to receive a compliment from the beautiful Lady Grace.

"All your life with him?" I asked. How come I've never met you? I've known him all my life too."

"It's a little complicated, yet simple at the same time. I am his real mother. Like your Grandma Lily who understands. Mothers are always with their children, physically or not. Jimmy was born in The Land of Possibilities and left when he was six months old for his mission. I have been with him, and all of you, the entire time you've known him. You just never saw me."

"Wow," was all I had. I remembered Jimmy telling me about leaving there when he was six months old, so I guess it all made some sense.

We then continued on the greatest thrill ride anyone could imagine. Man, the last time I had this much fun was when Jimmy and I were flying on Rufus's back. This was like defying gravity. Just going up and up, higher and higher, suspended in the air. I felt no fear whatsoever. Once I got used to it.

We were sailing up higher than I ever thought was humanly possible. There were clouds surrounding us everywhere. And the cherubs, man, they were singing furiously now. I was having the time of my life. I was ecstatic and overjoyed, but my joy could not surpass the joy I witnessed on the face of Grandma Lily. We were floating and had become one with the sky and the clouds. And to top it off, I was heading back to The Land of Possibilities and to possibly see Jimmy again!

After we'd been up in the sky for a good long while, we could no longer see each other, but we knew we were together because we were holding hands. As I'd said, I had one hand in the beautiful lady's and the other in Grandma Lily's. At one point I squeezed her hand really tightly and completely, and she squeezed back. It was euphoric. Finally, my dad would be complete and at peace.

THE LAND OF POSSIBILITIES: DAY 6

TWENTY-TWO

Jimmy felt really emotionally drained, although this had been a long time coming. It was why he'd been sent to be a friend and companion to Carol for the first part of her life. If she had not grown to trust him, she would never have asked him to accompany here to the club that day. Perhaps she'd have been okay on her own, but she may have run away when she'd realized what she'd be getting herself into.

Although there was nowhere to run once the bullets came. The Father always knew how to turn evil around for good for those who love him and the evil forces did not stand a chance. John had known they were going to be there and had shown up right on time. The bruises on his body were hard to look at but he had transformed himself to look like that for the memory. His heart had been broken to have seen him like that. However it was all in the past. It was very interesting to see Carol's face when she saw him and her reaction to the scars and his kind face. She had looked past the scars as few tend to do. If more were like her. However a lot of that would soon be a distant memory to her but she would not forget. Many will not believe her story or her grandmother's and no doubt they would have to stop trying to convince anyone.

It was all coming to heel. The entire mystery was going to be solved, and she'd never need to worry about her father and his emotional state and well-being again. Not that it'd been hers to worry about in the first place. Concerned was probably a better word. Most people on Earth had a tendency to worry and fret about much that they have no control over. For a while he'd been of them, well... except for the worry part. It had been interesting. He knew it would be hard to say goodbye to Carol. All she'd been through was still way beyond her grasp. The fact that he'd not return to Earth with her, she did not know yet, and he wondered how she'd handle the news.

His earthly parents already knew, so he'd have no explaining to do. In fact, everyone knew he didn't exist physically, except for Carol. How would she ever grasp the knowledge that he'd already been erased in the physical sense from the memories of all he'd spent time with down there? In their sixth sense, they would always feel his presence. Only Carol would know the difference. It was meant to be so.

It would be hardest for her. However, it would make her stronger and fulfill her earthly mission.

"Penny for your thoughts, son," joked Rufus, entering the living room where Jimmy was seated, cutting into his thoughts, as he always did. No trace of bird in sight, all man, wearing a beautiful casual white suit.

"Like you need it," Jimmy joked back. "Man-bird."

"Don't you call me that silly name, you know better," he said, transforming himself momentarily into man-bird for the sake of fun.

"The name suits you these days," said Jimmy, walking away to face the window and looking down.

"Have some fun at my expense, won't you, son?" he said.

Then looking at him intently, he asked. "Why so gloomy? You chose to go and no one forced you."

"I know," Jimmy replied.

"It was for love of Carol and the others as you already know. It was the ultimate mercy. I had to go."

"Do you think you'll miss it down there?"

"I won't miss it, no, but many will miss me. Miss knowing me. As you know, most have a need for me in the physical sense, to believe that I am truly present among them, and that will always sadden me. To many, I am already a distant memory, and soon I will be no more. Just like that! How can it be? It sometimes makes me wish the free will was not handed out so easily. So many would be better off without it, it seems."

"Never son, I tell you, never! It is only through free will that they can truly love, and that is the sacrifice. It is for the sake of love that free will was given, and there is nothing higher than that."

"Well said, Father. You are speaking my thoughts." Jimmy went over to him, and they exchanged a fierce hug. "Carol will soon be here," he said.

THE RETURN

A little while afterward, I began to feel our bodies descending and I could once more see the beautiful Lady and my Grandma, since we were no longer in the clouds. Soon thereafter, we landed in the beautiful mansion where the banquet had taken place. It felt serendipitous to be back there once more. Remember there was no roof so we just landed right in. The first person I saw was Jimmy and I couldn't have been anymore overjoyed! I was ecstatic to see my friend once again. Except there was something different, Jimmy radiated the brightest light I could ever have imagined. It was even brighter than the Great Light. How was that possible? It surrounded his entire body from head to toe. That didn't matter since for some reason it was not blinding me. "Jimmy!" I shouted, so excited to see him. I hugged him for as long as I could. I had so much to share with him in our time apart.

"You're here! I am so happy! I'd hoped you'd be here but there was no way I could know for sure. I've missed you so much! I know you did not abandon me and I was destined to have most of this long journey on my own. I know you would never desert me."

"You are right, dancer," said Jimmy lovingly.

"Did you receive my letter from The Great Light?"

"Yes—" Jimmy started to say...

I was too excited to let him finish. "I am so happy that you are still here. I was hoping nothing had happened to you but then

172

I should have known, since you have all those amazing powers I never knew of before. That should have made me know you'd be ok but it's so great to see for myself! And you are even brighter than The Great Light?"

To that Jimmy smiled. He looked so distinguished and nothing like the former Jimmy. He was wearing a beautiful robe again, like we were all wearing last time. Except his was an amazing violet color that, though I'm not that much into fashion but if I had to wear a color for the rest of my life that'd be it. And the sash that went with it shone like the brightest sun! I don't think we had any sashes the last time we were clothed in robes. Mental note.

I turned to look at Grandma Lily. "Look Jimmy, it's Grandma Lily! I found her!" I exclaimed, barely able to hold my excitement in—not that I was trying to. What a waste of effort that would be. "Well actually I happened to make it to where she was and the beautiful lady here, (I beckoned to Lady Grace)...brought her out from the most horribly smelling underground place."

Giving Lily his attention Jimmy turned to her and said, "Welcome to The Land of Possibilities, Lily. We are all sorry for the pain that you endured in The Valley of the Destitute."

"Thank you," she replied meekly, bowing. I was thinking, am I the only one who doesn't bow to Jimmy? This is still a strange concept to me. "It was the most horrible time, but just knowing I would one day be here and see your face was the only thing that made it bearable and I am just so grateful and to see my granddaughter in person for the first time is so beautiful. She's so beautiful and loving," she said, turning towards me.

"Oh stop Grandma," I said comically. I do not take compliments well.

Ignoring my response completely, "I know," said Jimmy. "Your granddaughter never gave up hope on helping you be free to go, either. Her faith has helped you get here sooner than expected."

Grandma Lily smiled ever so sweetly. "Thank you for always being her friend and at her side."

Jimmy nodded in acknowledgment of her genuineness. "It's what I do." So caught up in being reunited with Jimmy I was unaware of anyone else in the palace. I'd almost forgotten about Lady Grace as well, but I shouldn't have worried. She appeared to have vanished.

"Welcome back, Carol!" said a much familiar voice. Turning around, I expected to see Rufus, but instead I saw my tree! The sight of it brought me ecstasy. I loved that tree. It was my friend, and had been my lone companion when I'd woken up at the river. Only difference was—well, this time it was talking. However, nothing surprises me anymore. Except, man, it had a face. Rufus' face!

"Man-bird?" for a moment I let my old term of reference for Rufus slip out.

"Man-bird? Child, I stand before you as a tree, am I not?"

With that, I burst into laughter—and so did everyone else, for that matter. He sure was entertaining.

"So, it was you with me when I woke up at the river?" I asked incredulously.

"For shizzle," he replied. We all burst into hysterical laughter again. This time we were joined by the beautiful Lady, who had mysteriously reappeared. I'd know that sweet laughter anywhere. Things couldn't get any better. I was reunited with Jimmy, and would be bringing Grandma Lily home to my dad. I had to pinch myself once again to verify that this wasn't a dream. I did so secretly. I didn't think anyone actually did that, and it was only something they said, but I didn't care. I'd been through too much in the past five days. I deserved to be a little wacky.

Grandma Lily stood there agape at the talking tree.

Suddenly, Lady Grace approached me. I wondered where she'd been since I hadn't seen her for a while. "Hi Lady Grace, sorry with so much going on I forgot about you, not really forgot but I was caught up ..."

"No apologies necessary dear," she replied smiling gently.

"Thank you for everything. I am so grateful to you for rescuing my grandmother. I will never be able to repay your kindness, if I lived a million years.

Lady Grace raised her hand, placing her finger on her lips as if to shush me and walked towards me. As she drew near she reached down from her ten foot frame and placed a beautiful gemmed tiara on my head. It was made of white diamonds and pearls just like Mustafa had said.

I was speechless for a moment. I obviously hadn't bought into the royalty thing the Mustafa and the teenage angels had tried to convince me of in The Valley of The Destitute.

"Wow! What's going on?" I asked when I got my tongue back.

"It is no longer invisible to you," she said, smiling.

Shortly after, she also placed an exact replica on my Grandma Lily's head. Grandma Lily seemed to have handled hers better. She curtsied to Lady Grace and just looked at her enthralled.

THE DECISION

TWENTY-THREE

"Well, Lily," said Rufus. "What is your decision?" Decision, I thought. I wondered what decision Grandma Lily needed to make. I turned around to Rufus. For the first time I saw him in full body. I was stunned. He was wearing a gorgeous blue suit.

"Don't be distracted by the get up," he said when he saw my stunned look. I am real too. I am also Jimmy's real father."

"Oh?" Was all I could get out, turning to look at Jimmy who nodded his head and smiled.

I didn't know what to say.

"Yes, Carol. It will be Lily's decision to stay here, or return with you to Berkeley Springs. You know, things are not too bad here in The Land of Possibilities. She may wish to stay," Rufus continued.

"I know how beautiful it is here," I said, panic mode in high gear, by now gotten over the news of Jimmy's birth father. "But…my dad needs her! He never got to know her since he was a little boy and he's always so sad, and—" I was getting breathless. I was not expecting this new development.

"Say you'll go with me Grandma Lily. Please, say you will!" I was close to tears. My heart was breaking. Goes to show you how things could change in the blink of an eye, to utter despair from my joy minutes ago. Now, all could change based on Grandma Lily's reply.

"You know, if she returns with you, there's a possibility she could end up again in that horrible place she just got out from, Carol. You've only had just an inkling of what that place is like.

179

Pray you never end up there yourself. If Lily decides to return with you, there's no guarantee to her that she won't go back there again. It's a tough decision for her to make. You must accept whatever she decides, dear."

I knew he made sense. I wouldn't wish that place Grandma Lily had just escaped from on anyone. The room was absolutely quiet. We were all waiting for Grandma Lily to give her answer.

"I'd like to return with Carol and get to be with my son Marc and his beautiful family. My daughter in law Miriam and my grandson Jeremy. I know one day we will all be back here in The Land Of possibilities. I have faith and believe this to be so but right now on Earth my son needs me," replied Lily as she gave Carol a wink.

I was ecstatic! "Thank you, Grandma Lily," I said, reaching for her hand and squeezing it tightly.

I had many questions for Grandma Lily. I wanted to have some time alone with her. So I asked, "I would like to have some time alone with my grandma, please," I said to no one in particular.

"Sure, my child," replied the beautiful Lady. However, remember you will have plenty of time to catch up and get answers to all your questions when you both return to Earth."

"That's true, but what if—"

"Yes?" said man-bird, eyeing me cautiously. Immediately our last trust conversation came to mind.

"Okay, no what ifs. But still..." I said quickly.

"You may have some time alone with her, but don't forget you'll both be leaving shortly," he said.

With those words, they all vanished, and Grandma Lily and I were alone. I didn't know where to begin, but I needed to know how she'd ended up in the Land of the Destitute.

"I know you have many questions, and I will try to tell you as honestly and truthfully as I can in the short time we have. It may be a little hard to stomach some of it so be prepared. More will be revealed to you in time when we return and spend more time together.

"However here's a little summary. When your dad was six years old, your Grandfather David and I were taken captive by some very bad people. On our last day together, the three of us were out in a meadow, having a beautiful day and a picnic."

"My dream, I saw it!"

"You did?" she said excitedly.

"Yes, you were all so happy!"

"Yes, we were. So, that was our last happy day. The part you didn't see. Probably your guardian angel must have blocked it out and woke you up," she smiled. "It was shortly after when toward sunset, the men came from the bush and demanded money from David in exchange for our lives. He gave them everything he had. However, it wasn't enough. There were four men and two of them took your dad and the other two blindfolded me. I could hear your dad and David screaming and shortly after an engine revved and took off. I was blindfolded all the way to that horrible club Monet where I was kept captive." Grandma Lily took a breath as she continued. I could tell reliving the story was really tearing her apart. "My poor darlings," she sobbed.

"How terrible!" I cried out passionately.

"I cried for them day and night for three months, although sometimes I had to, secretly for fear of my captives and their lack of empathy," continued Grandma Lily.

"So dad ended up in an orphanage when he was six. I guess everyone presumed you dead. I heard my parents speaking of dad growing up in the orphanage one night when I was small and went into their room in the middle of the night. I knew the truth, though, that at least you were alive. And what of Grandfather David?"

"I have no idea, my child. Perhaps he was never found or his body was."

"I had those dreams…"

"Dreams are good, Carol, especially yours. Your dad must have tried to tell those people at the orphanage the truth. He was only six. They probably had no clues on where to find me and he probably gave up. My poor boy," she said, breaking out into fresh sobs. I too started weeping for my six-year-old father.

"Sorry Grandma Lily. You don't have to go on," I said sympathetically.

"No, it's okay dear," she said, sighing heavily and wiping the tears from her eyes. "It's important to know the truth. The truth is, my David…" she continued bravely. "Your grandfather did unfortunately go to Iraq. I detest wars of any kind."

"Me too," I agreed.

"He went for about one year, but due to a leg injury, he was discharged and returned home. During his absence my mother, your great grandmother, my beautiful mother Mary was killed in a tragic hit and run. I was devastated. When David returned he was my rock. We were married for eight glorious years," she said ecstatically. "Until the incident in the meadow. After the incident for many months those terrible people held me captive in Club Monet, and though I tried to escape many times, my efforts were all futile. I was desperate to find your dad and David and have my family. They always caught me. They were involved in drugs and wild parties and everything vile. After a while towards the three month period I gave up on trying to escape and I became corrupted like the others. One afternoon I went down into the wine cellar and they started shooting at me.

"Yes, us too!" I yelled.

She gave me a surprised look and continued. I couldn't see where the bullets were from but I saw a guy standing there with scars and a kind face who told me to run fast and I did and then next thing I know I was in the Valley of the Destitute. As bad as it was I was happy to be out of The Club Monet because there were no drugs and all those bad parties and everyone always spoke of The Land of Possibilities that we would go to.

"Club Monet is now a rundown abandoned place. Maybe they were found out and were all thrown in jail."

"Perhaps so. I have no idea what became of my dear David, your grandfather. I tried all I could to find out," she said sadly.

I couldn't hear anymore. This was too painful.

"Stop!" I shouted to her. "I've heard enough." I began to sob loudly.

"My child, it is all in the past now. Be happy. We have much to be grateful and happy for," she said, breaking into a smile. I realized how I'd missed my dad. Her smile was exactly like his.

"Even more," said a strange voice.

We were both startled and turned around instantaneously. I couldn't believe it. I recognized him instantly. It was my Grandfather David. I knew him from the dream!

"David!" Grandma Lily cried out in astonishment as they reached out for and ran towards each other and embraced.

"Grandpa!" I yelled out, running toward them both. Well, I wasn't about to be left out. Group hug. We all three hugged for again what seemed like an eternity.

My grandma had never looked more beautiful, staring up at my Grandpa David. Now there was a woman with some questions. He must have read her mind.

"I've been here in The Land of Possibilities, waiting for you for quite some time Lily, Ever since that horrible incident in the meadow." he said. At which she broke down in tears.

"You were always so good... no wonder you are here."

"Yes, I did, but not a second went by that I wished I could have exchanged places to ease your pain, my dear Lily. But it wasn't for me to do," he said sadly.

"I've been here waiting for you. I'm so sorry I couldn't stop them my Lily and all the pain they caused you."

"Thank you. I know you would have if you could," she replied with a joyful look. You did your best."

"Thank you my love. It was all God's will and I learned to accept that and I guess he wanted me home sooner in The Land of Possibilities."

"Yes darling, he must have," replied Grandma Lily. "It's all behind us now and I forgive them."

"That's the spirit my love!" said my grandfather jubilantly.

"Still want to return with Carol?" asked Lady Grace to my grandmother.

"Can my grandfather return with us?" I asked, hoping it could be so.

"Unfortunately, he can't dear," said the beautiful Lady Grace with a heavy sigh.

"Yes, Lily, I've waited for you so long now, and I'll wait forever. Our son needs you," said Grandpa David. "He'll have me too, in time. I'll be right here waiting for all of you."

At this my Grandma Lily broke into a big grin. "Thank you, my dear David. I'll be back soon and I'll do much better this time," she said, hugging him tightly.

My bedtime story finally laid to rest.

Suddenly, I noticed almost everyone I'd met on my journey beginning from Club Monet was in the castle with us. The man in the wine cellar, how'd he get here...so he was also involved too? Figures. His face was beautiful as before and there were no visible scars. Didn't surprise me...those probably disappeared in The Land of Possibilities. He winked when he saw me look at him. I smiled. Jimmy saw us exchange looks and said to me, "That's John."

For a moment the picture of him in the wine cellar came rushing back and Jimmy and I exchanged a soulful look. It had all been a plan.

I kept looking around. There was Rufus, The Great Light, Lady Grace and the cherubim. Also the singing flying girls, I finally figured out were seraphim. My guardian angel Sage who I saw was standing right next to me smiling, I smiled back of course, the other guardians Jasmine and Rose. Then I also saw Mustafa who winked at me! I winked back with happy laughter. It was a happy moment I'd treasure forever. I even saw the unicorns looking so peaceful for a change. They didn't look like they were ready to take off. They must be on a rest break. I blinked when my last ride I'd bonded with smiled at me. That was too cool. I grinned from ear to ear. There were over a hundred or so other people all over the castle, and they all looked so distinguished and royal. At that moment crowns and tiaras appeared on all of their heads. It was so amazing! Jimmy, Lady Grace and Rufus's crowns shone the brightest and were bigger than the others. That told me a lot. It told me all. Everything was now crystal clear and I had no more questions. Many of the people were also sitting on beautiful brocade chairs that looked a lot like thrones, including Jimmy.

"We promise we'll be with you both every moment, even when you can't see me," stepped in Jimmy, my wonderful friend, as we walked away from his throne. "In many ways it will be better."

"Thank you, Jimmy, I said as I half bowed, half curtsied to him (I hadn't had much practice in that area). I had now joined the ranks of the flying girl cherubim in bowing to my friend. "You are the best friend, I will always love you. I am also very happy you are home here with your true parents in The Land of Possibilities where all is indeed possible," I said exuberantly, as we hugged tightly.

"Be love," Jimmy answered back. His last words to me.

❀❀❀

"Jump on!" yelled Rufus returning in his man bird splendor once again. I already knew what to do, so I showed Grandma Lily the ropes. He beckoned to Sage. Who immediately vanished! I had an idea where to, except I could no longer see him. I wondered if I'd actually be able to see him again. I also wondered what Grandma Lily's guardian angel looked like as we took off, as I now knew for sure we all have a guardian angel and it's not just some story. Then we took off from the palace and said goodbye to The Land Of Possibilities. I waved at Jimmy, Lady Grace and all the others. Rufus flew us back in about two minutes to our same start off point. The disgraced Club Monet. Better than landing on a yellow cab I think. I really would not like to go through what that little boy on ET went through. On landing in the Club Monet, through a tiny window that Rufus had downsized his gigantic being to enter, we'd found it completely deserted, of course. Was I surprised? Not really. I'd seen and heard too much those past seven days. Grandma Lily shivered when we landed in The Club Monet but she handled it quite well. I noticed her tiara was gone. I reached up and touched my head. It was also bare. Guess they didn't survive the ride. We bade a teary goodbye to Rufus. He looked sad as a single tear drop fell from one of his eyes, then hugged us both with his huge wings. "Thank you Rufus, I sure will miss you," I said as my grandma Lily looked on. "Don't you worry dear," he replied as he wiped his tear off his face. We will meet again." He smiled at us both then vanished right before our very eyes.

We stood there for a couple minutes in awe, and then ran outside to board the subway on 42nd street. First thing I saw when we arrived at the entrance was a pair of purple cowboy boots. Greg! How did he know?

THE END

EPILOGUE

EARTH

Three months later:

I've been back home from New York for three months now and my dad's been happier than I'd ever hoped to see in my wildest imagination. It was an incredible transformation. The sad look in his eyes is completely gone. Now my joy is complete! He and Grandma Lily spend all waking moments catching up. It's beautiful. She has settled in with us quite nicely. We all just love her and she and Jeremy are firm friends. You should have been a fly on the wall five months ago, when Grandpa Dwayne and Grandma Julie made their first non-Christmas visit that I can remember. What a reunion.

My Grandma Lily, my mom and I know everything that's happened. Oh, Godmother Lady Hall too, of course. They've tried to explain it all to me and my dad. I'm glad we don't have any secrets anymore. Jeremy doesn't really care how she got here. He's just happy she is. As for me, I prefer to think of it all as a wild dream, though I know better.

I will return to New York and join Brittany, Karen and Greg in the fall. No doubt I'll be lagging behind, but not for too long. Greg has promised not to get too far ahead, so I won't feel too lame. What a guy!

Brittany and Karen have never asked of Jimmy. It was just as he'd said. It's like he never existed. Greg didn't ask about him either. Later, I'd also remembered Jimmy saying he'd told them that I'd be gone for a while. He'd never said we. So as weird as it all was, maybe it all added up. When my Grandma Lily and I had run into Greg at the subway, he'd said that he'd just happened to be there. I was only gone for three hours, I found out. The six days had never even occurred back on earth. I introduced Grandma Lily to Greg and he was so happy I'd found her. I tried to explain what had happened to Greg but he gave me a weird look. Grandma Lily said nothing. She was the smart one. I had no better luck with the twins. I believe they would have planned an intervention if my grandmother and I hadn't left for home as soon as we did. Grandma Lily however, had backed me up and eventually they gave up and accepted our story as crazy as it was. Perhaps they were all in on it anyway and were just pretending. I'd ridden that train before. My grandma bought Greg some new boots and although he could have had any other color, he insisted he needed another purple pair. She'd taken all of us on a shopping spree before we left Manhattan for Berkeley Springs. She'd still had a bank account with funds in Manhattan. She said it should have been closed by now but somehow it was still open. So far that's been the only weird occurrence back on earth. We spent three days packing and then boarded our plane home. When we got home and our story came to light, missing persons contacted us. When we told them our story, they thought we were either hiding something or coo coo for cocoa puffs.

I decided not to say anything about any of it anymore. The Land Of Possibilities truly existed. I believed in my heart that it'd been Heaven. I remembered that clearly registering just before we departed. It had been a complete and utter realization. Although for some weird reason the entire time I was there before then the thought hadn't even occurred. I truly had been clueless or didn't want to think it was possible.

I believed it to have been Heaven now not just because of the angels (since angels, though mostly unseen on earth, are here). It was way deeper. Although no one the entire time had said who they really were by the actual names. I knew and that's all that mattered. I'd also been to Hell (The Isle of The Hopeless) and Purgatory (The Valley of The Destitute). I knew that truth deep in my soul. Though how Grandma Lily was able to leave purgatory and return with me was truly unexplainable. But we can't put God in a box since He's in charge and He did ask her if she wanted to return. I knew who Jimmy had had to have been. He'd been Jesus! I know, weird. Oh, but how amazing! And I know who I believed Rufus and Lady Grace were, too. God the Father was Rufus and Lady Grace, Mary. The Great Light must have been Saint Michael the Archangel and the beautiful Saint John was the one who'd had the scars. I am not sure which John he was, since there are more than one (smile). I hadn't seen Saint Peter (that I know of) and since that's his duty, he must have opened the tiny little gate.

However, when folks in our neighborhood now ask me how I'd found my Grandma Lily. I'd made a decision to keep it simple.

My answer to them "If I told you the whole story you wouldn't believe me. So I'll make it short. I had some help from my friend, A New York Crazy."

However at some point I wish one day to tell Jeremy I'd seen chickens in Heaven and Dale could have been one of them.

AUTHOR'S NOTE

A few years ago, I received the news of the loss of a young family member. When I got the news it hit me like a ten foot pole. I had never experienced anything like it before. Although I am of the belief that all of us are passing through and this world is certainly not our home, my young relative's passing from this life, weighed heavily on my mind and heart. Oftentimes, with tragedy it is our reaction that matters most and our loved ones gone do expect us to move on and let go.

That same week, I delved into writing this little novel, *'The Land of Possibilities 'The Search for Grandma Lily.'* It was definitely an emotional outlet and I couldn't stop writing. Once I started there were healings in so many aspects of my life up to that point, I could not have imagined. I started having fun with all my characters and they became dear friends! I knew each one deeply. And I hope you will too!

Please always do remember there is always a creative outlet of choice available to all of us if and or whenever the need arises.

For me, I realized how fragmented our families are at times, and sometimes we all seem at a loss to fix. While it plays out, our comfort is, or should be, that one day things will be different and all pure hearts will be revealed.

Land of Possibilities is a fictional novel yet it is based on some aspects of what I consider my truth. It is serious and funny at the same time, as is life. Though it may appeal more to teens, it is also for all... and the not so faint at heart!

The Land of Possibilities: Search for Grandma Lily will remind all of us that nothing is impossible with God.

-Seren Hart

AUTHOR LINKS

'*THE LAND OF POSSIBILITIES* WAS WRITTEN TO BE
READ BY ALL'

If you love and enjoyed reading *The Land of Possibilities* '*the
search for Grandma Lily*' please pass the news along and share this
little story of love, hope and enchantment...
Order as a gift to your teens, friends and family, for your
church, your book club or if you own a shop or storefront consider
putting a display of *Land Of Possibilities* for resell...
Write a book review and like and follow on 'The Land of
Possibilities, The Search For Grandma Lily' and 'Seren Hart
Author' social sites. You may also write a review on other book
websites you frequent and your favorite magazines or local
newspapers.
If you have a blog consider writing on how you have enjoyed
reading the *Land of Possibilities* ...but don't give too much away!
You may ask your favorite radio show or podcast to have the
author on as a guest...
The author would love to meet you...contact her for any
charitable or fundraising event for your church, group, school or
charity...

And follow...
www.facebook.com/serenhartauthor
www.thelandofpossibilities.com
www.serenhart.com
https://twitter.com/serenhartauthor